Lady Mary's Dangerous Encounter

The Beresford Adventures
Book 1

Cheryl Bolen

© Copyright 2021 by Cheryl Bolen
Text by Cheryl Bolen
Cover by Wicked Smart Designs

Dragonblade Publishing, Inc. is an imprint of Kathryn Le Veque Novels, Inc.
P.O. Box 7968
La Verne CA 91750
ceo@dragonbladepublishing.com

Produced in the United States of America

First Edition July 2021
Trade Paperback Edition

Reproduction of any kind except where it pertains to short quotes in relation to advertising or promotion is strictly prohibited.

All Rights Reserved.

The characters and events portrayed in this book are fictitious. Any similarity to real persons, living or dead, is purely coincidental and not intended by the author.

ARE YOU SIGNED UP FOR DRAGONBLADE'S BLOG?

You'll get the latest news and information on exclusive giveaways, exclusive excerpts, coming releases, sales, free books, cover reveals and more.

Check out our complete list of authors, too!

No spam, no junk. That's a promise!

Sign Up Here

www.dragonbladepublishing.com

Dearest Reader;

Thank you for your support of a small press. At Dragonblade Publishing, we strive to bring you the highest quality Historical Romance from the some of the best authors in the business. Without your support, there is no 'us', so we sincerely hope you adore these stories and find some new favorite authors along the way.

Happy Reading!

CEO, Dragonblade Publishing

Additional Dragonblade books by Author Cheryl Bolen

The Beresford Adventures
Lady Mary's Dangerous Encounter (Book 1)
My Lord Protector (Book 2)

PROLOGUE

W HY IN THE devil had Devere summoned Stephen to his formidable house on Curzon Street today? Except for a passing nod at White's, the two men hadn't communicated with one another since their days at Oxford a decade ago.

The note Stephen had received this morning from his old university friend said he needed to discuss an urgent matter.

Lord Stephen Stanhope was still pondering this perplexing question as he handed off his hat, coat, and muffler to the Devere butler.

"My master regrets that he will have to entertain you in his bedchamber, owing to his infirmity."

Stephen's brows lowered. "What is the nature of his lordship's infirmity?"

"The poor fellow was climbing a tree at Hamberly to fetch Lady Harriett's kitten when the branch that bore his weight broke." The white-haired retainer shook his head morosely. "Nasty break. He's having to keep the leg elevated, and my lord has been in considerable pain."

Such pain Stephen understood. He, too, had broken his leg when he was a cocky lad who thought he could break in a most unmanageable filly.

As he and the butler mounted an iron-banistered staircase that curved to the first floor, long-dead Devere ancestors stared down at them from portraits. Even though Stephen's own father was a duke, their London home could not rival the richness of Devere House.

From the lavishly furnished drawing room they reached a corridor—with more dead ancestor portraits—that led to Devere's private chambers.

"Good of you to come," Devere greeted as Stephen stepped into the masculine chamber. The earl sat up in the center of a massive full-tester bed, his waxed and leather-sheathed leg propped on a mound of pillows. The earl was two years older than Stephen but had about him a boyish countenance perpetrated by his carelessly styled hair and his propensity to smile. Though he was not smiling today.

A fire blazing at the marble hearth kept the room warm, and a half a dozen tall windows cloaked in the same royal blue silk as the bed would have brightened the chamber were it not so dreary a November day.

The butler left, closing the door behind him.

"Please sit." Devere waved at an armchair between the bed and the windows.

"Sorry about your leg, old fellow. Beastly painful, I know from experience."

A grim look on his face, Devere nodded. "The blasted thing is prohibiting me from doing anything." He frowned. "And there's a bit of a family crisis I'm hoping you can help with."

A family crisis? Stephen could not fathom how he could help in such a situation. "I'd be happy to assist you, but I leave the country tomorrow."

"That's precisely why I need you. I understand you're to replace Lord Ellsworthy at the Congress of Vienna."

Few people knew of Ellsworthy's ill health or that Stephen had been dispatched from the Foreign Office to replace him. Devere obviously had friends at the highest levels of government.

"You're well informed. And you've certainly piqued my interest."

"What I'm going to tell you is in the strictest confidence, and I'm counting on your gentlemanly discretion to protect my sister's reputation."

"Lady Sophia?"

Devere shook his head. "No. Thankfully, Sophia's happily wed to one of those frightfully rich Birminghams. I no longer have to worry about her." He sighed. "It's Maryann—my most exasperating sister. She's possessed of the most tender heart, and we dearly love her, but she's always been . . . exceedingly headstrong. She confidently barrels into situations that end up overwhelming her. The girl takes it upon herself to do the most outrageous things."

"Such as?"

"Last year, she thought it was her duty to rescue common streetwalkers from their sordid lives." Devere rolled his eyes. "She would bring them into our home as if they were stray pups. Allow me to say, they were not the influence I would have chosen for my maiden sisters. Telling my hard-headed sister I would not tolerate such intervention was like talking to one of my youngest sister's cats." He shrugged. "Maryann tends to ignore my sage advice. It wasn't until Sophia intervened that we were able to rid our home of those disreputable women—and then only because an inordinate number of valuable items kept turning up missing. Still, Maryann insisted on trying to rehabilitate the . . . ladies."

"Very commendable."

"She's a lovely person—but most vexing." He sighed. "Another of her foibles is that she . . . how can I put this delicately? She is ruled by a dramatic flair and is given to . . . to stretch the truth. Truth, to her, is boring. She can take a root of truth and feed it with her lively imagination, making it into something far more interesting. In her eyes."

Stephen was gratified it was Devere—and not himself—who was responsible for such an incorrigible girl. It made him appreciate his own staid sisters all the more. "I perceive that Lady

Maryann has once again exasperated you."

A pained expression on his face, Devere nodded. "I'm terrified for her safety."

"What has she done now?"

"I forbade her to travel to Vienna to visit Sophia." Wincing, Devere reached for a paper on the bedside table. "Yesterday morning I received this note."

My Dearest Brother,

Please do not worry about me. I have decided that since I am now one-and-twenty, I no longer need your permission to undertake the journey to Vienna. Since you will not permit me to use one of the Devere coaches, I shall travel there alone, hiring public vehicles as I go. I shan't trouble you for money as I have saved rather a lot. It will be a great adventure, and I am most capable of seeing to my own needs.

I remain out of charity with you but love you nevertheless.

Mary

Were one of Stephen's younger sisters to have the audacity to strike off on her own across the Continent, he'd be sorely tempted to lock her up indefinitely—after racing across the Continent to catch up with the maddening girl. "She's only one-and-twenty?"

Devere nodded solemnly.

"I can certainly see why you're alarmed. It's exceedingly dangerous for a young woman to be traveling across the Continent alone. Surely she's brought along servants?"

His expression even more pained, Devere shook his head.

"I don't suppose you can hope she is . . . homely?"

"I could hope she was homely, but unfortunately she's quite lovely. And I'm not saying that because of brotherly partiality." He reached once more toward his bedside table. "Here is her miniature."

Stephen peered at the tiny oval painting that depicted a delicate blonde with perfect ivory complexion and large pale blue eyes. She was stunning. "I can see why you're terrified. She's beautiful."

As small-boned as she was, the poor girl would be incapable of fighting off any threat.

"I beg that you keep it," Devere said. "I know you're to attend the Congress of Vienna, and I am begging you to find—and protect—my sister during her journey. I appeal to you as an old friend and as a brother, too, of maiden sisters. I propose to provide you with sufficient funds for your journey. Because you're a younger son and because of your father's financial setbacks, I believe you might welcome, shall we say, five-hundred pounds."

It was an enormous sum—almost twice Stephen's meager annual income. He could certainly use it.

But he would not accept a farthing from so distressed a man. He shook his head. "I couldn't take your money. I tremble just thinking of one of my sisters being off alone like that." *Though none of my sisters would ever be that foolish.* "Besides, you were a kind upperclassman to me when I first came to Oxford. I will do my best to find your sister."

Stephen stood. "Do you have any clues about what route she might have taken?"

Devere shrugged. "All I know is that my sister is enamored of William Beckford's travel journal."

Stephen's brows lowered. "I thought he'd had most copies destroyed."

"He did. My father was fortunate to have received one of the copies before the bonfire."

"I suppose Lady Maryann took it with her?"

"Unfortunately. I only know of one other edition. At the Bodleian in Oxford."

Stephen didn't have time to travel to Oxford. "I shall see if Lord Harley has a copy."

"If anyone in London does, it would be Harley."

Being the son of a duke, even an impoverished duke, had its advantages. Stephen had access to the country's most noble families. And, hopefully, their libraries.

"If I should be fortunate enough to catch up with your sister . . ."

"I'd rather you not say I requested you to follow her."

Stephen nodded.

"And there's one more thing," Devere said.

Stephen turned around.

"My sister has recently taken it into her head to shorten her name from Maryann to Mary."

Stephen had already observed how she'd signed the note to her brother. Devere had his sympathy. Stephen thanked God Lady Mary was not his sister. "Good to know."

CHAPTER ONE

L ADY MARYANN BERESFORD had made it a lifelong habit to never own up to her rash actions, to never admit she could possibly be wrong. Such unwarranted arrogance could likely be attributed to the fact she was the middle daughter. She believed it impossible to compete with the eldest Beresford daughter—the gorgeous, perfect Lady Sophia—nor could she compete for lovability with Harriett, the adorable youngest daughter. Therefore, Maryann had made it a practice to call attention to her flamboyant self by oozing with the confidence of One Who Knows All.

Today, though, as she waited for the cadre of warmly bundled Swiss porters to dismantle her hired coach for the arduous journey across the Alps, she admitted to herself that her clothing was frightfully inadequate against this brutal chill. The coldest Yorkshire winters of her youth in no way prepared her for these frigid howling alpine winds that dripped with a perpetual mist.

Woolen stockings, flannel undergarments, a merino dress, woolen pelisse, and heavy hooded velvet cloak were as ineffective against this savage cold as an umbrella in a monsoon. At least her hands, sheathed in snug kid gloves and tucked within a mammoth ermine muff, were warm. For that, she was profoundly thankful.

A pity she hadn't purchased beaver outer garments like the porters wore. If these hulking giants weren't so exceedingly tall, she would have been sorely tempted to disrobe one in order to seize his warm outerwear. What in the devil did they feed these oversized Swiss? To a man, each of them looked as if he ingested an entire cow at every meal.

What a pity she had forced herself to ignore the lure of Holland's windmills and canals—all for naught—in order to reach the Alps before winter paralyzed all activity here. Surely January couldn't possibly be worse than this glacial early December day.

She had thought she'd prepared well for the journey by reading William Beckford's account of his Grand Tour so many times she knew most passages by heart. She had brought personal locks to secure her chamber doors, essential oil of lavender to drive bugs from the dubious bedding of roadside inns, a stash of tea, a passport holder stamped with the Devere crest, remedies against motion sickness (which she had almost depleted), wax candles for the coach lamps, and many notebooks in which to scribble her impressions of the foreign lands that had for so long beckoned to her.

She had also read that it would be necessary to bring a penknife to assist one when eating. It could also serve as a weapon, if needed, Mary reasoned, confident in her own resourcefulness.

Lady Mary's thirst to travel across the Continent had been fed not only by journals of the enormously rich Beckford but also by a sizable number of other accounts written by English travelers.

She rather fancied publishing her own book after this journey. While she stood there curiously watching her coach being reduced to small parts and loaded onto mules, her face stinging from the cold, she imagined the celebrity she would enjoy once her travel journal was published to acclaim.

With her fame established by her wildly successful book, she could see herself traveling to the Orient and becoming known as the intrepid, worldly Lady Mary Beresford. She would wear silken veils and dangling jewels and would ride upon camels along vast deserts amidst swaying palm trees.

A warm desert held vast appeal right now! No matter how

much she concentrated upon images of endless sands, she still shivered with cold and saw nothing but mounds of white snow.

Her reverie halted when a young man whose neck was disfigured by a bulging goiter struggled to lift her trunk of books.

Speaking in flawless French, she suggested he get another man to assist as the books were exceedingly heavy. He offered her a shy smile, and then speaking in a curious blend of French, Italian and German, he begged the assistance of an older man.

Those writers of travel journals had most certainly lied when they'd said these mountain passes were populated with British travelers. It had been days since she'd seen a fellow Brit. How she longed to speak in her native tongue, though her old governess would swear French was as much her native tongue as English. She had learned both simultaneously while still in leading strings, and nothing but French had ever been spoken at the Devere dinner table.

Because she did not possess sufficient command of the German language, she was relieved that the world leaders convening in Vienna would be speaking in French, the language of diplomacy.

How fortunate her sister Sophia was to be married to such a man of the world as Will Birmingham. In the short time she'd been married, Sophia had the good fortune of residing in Paris, traveling to Venice, and now made her home in Vienna, where her husband was looking after the Birmingham banking interest. Mary could not wait to see the glittering palaces and opera houses of the Hapsburgs.

It was a strong lament of Mary's that none of the Englishmen with whom she was acquainted shared her affinity for foreign travel. Perhaps that explained why she was still unwed. She refused to marry until she found a man as attracted to faraway places as she.

A wee little girl clad in the flimsiest dress imaginable emerged from a nearby hovel whose roof was so close to the ground Mary doubted that these towering men could stand to their full heights inside.

Because it appeared the child's matted blonde hair had not been touched by a brush in a considerable period of time and because of the forlorn look on her gaunt little face, Mary suspected she was motherless.

Mary's heart went out to the shivering creature. Nary a glove protected the poor child's reddened hands, and her feet were shod in well-worn shoes that were much too large. Her big, solemn green eyes fixed longingly upon Mary's magnificent ermine muff. Shyly, she approached Mary, and her tiny hand stroked the muff's soft pelt. A smile brightened that melancholy face.

It fairly broke Mary's heart. "Here," Mary said in French, handing the muff to the child.

The girl tentatively inserted her frigid hands and looked up at Mary with a grateful smile.

"It's yours. Take it," Mary said ruefully. She knew she would come to regret her impetuous generosity, but there you have it. She would not have hesitated to repeat the offer.

At the sound of an approaching coach, the child looked up, her face once again turning solemn. Then her little legs whisked her—and Mary's beautiful muff—back to the hovel from which she had come.

Mary's gaze followed the coach. As it came close enough to identify, her face hardened, and she turned away. The vehicle bore the distinctive markings of a French carriage maker. Mary despised the French. Even though Napoleon had been exiled to Elba, her loathing of his megalomania ran deep. And because she was an aristocrat, she abhorred the French efforts to annihilate their blue-blooded countrymen.

Moments later, a lone passenger from the French coach approached her and spoke in English. "How gratifying it is to find another Englishwoman here in the Alps."

Mary whirled around to face the bespectacled speaker. As small as Mary was, this woman was even smaller. With her stooped shoulders and silver hair, she appeared to be in her sixties. "How ever did you know I'm English?" Mary asked.

The older woman shrugged. "I've been so long from my homeland that I've learned to spot a fellow Brit from fifty paces. Have you ever noticed the French women all have the same way of dressing?"

"I will own, I am not much acquainted with Frenchwomen."

"I have now lived among them for more years than I lived in the country of my birth." The woman, who had the advantage on Mary because she had wisely dressed in beaver hat, coat, boots and gloves, curtsied. "I am Miss Agatha Willets."

Now Mary knew two things about the woman. Her spinsterhood had been confirmed, and her voice indicated she was genteel born.

Mary smiled. "I'm massively grateful to meet you, Miss Willets. I am Lady Mary Beresford." Mary had only recently shortened her Christian name from Maryann, deeming Mary far more mature sounding. "I've despaired of ever seeing anyone from my homeland."

The spinster's brows lowered. "Beresford? Is your father the Earl of Devere?"

"He was. My brother has now succeeded him."

"I am very sorry to hear of your dear father's passing."

"You knew him?"

"A little. When I was a girl in Oxford, my father tutored him. I was quite in awe of the handsome fellow. In addition to his good looks, he was exceedingly well mannered. He was a great favorite of my father's."

"He was a dear, and I'm happy to say all of his good qualities have passed to my brother."

Mary could not help but to wonder how the spinster daughter of a tutor came to be traveling in a costly carriage crossing the Alps.

"To where do you travel, Lady Mary?" the jolly little woman asked.

"I'm going to visit my sister in Vienna."

The old woman's wrinkled face brightened. "As am I!" She giggled. "Not to see your sister. To go to Vienna, I mean. I'm a governess. I've spent my life imparting knowledge to French children, and since my last charges have quite grown up, I've now been recommended as governess to the children of a French diplomat attending the Congress of Vienna. Monsieur d'Arblay was kind enough to send one of his splendid coaches to convey me there." Mist gathered on her lashes as she squinted at Mary. "Surely, my dear, you are not traveling alone."

"But I am. Much to my brother's chagrin, I am resolutely independent."

"I do fear for your safety. You're far too young and too pretty."

The always-confident Mary was incapable of experiencing fear. "Having never before left England, I'm much too exhilarated to be afraid of anything."

"I suppose your brother did ensure that you'd be protected by armed postilions and faithful retainers."

"Actually, I've hired a coach and must trust that these men are reliable. I am possessed of a most trusting nature."

Miss Willets glared. "Is that wise, do you think?"

Mary gave a false laugh. "You sound exactly like Devere."

"I must say I am delighted that we'll be rather together in our travels. It will be safer for both of us."

***

IT WAS FORTUNATE, Stephen thought, that Lady Maryann—at least at the start of her journey—had followed the itinerary William Beckford had established back in 1780. It was fortunate, too, that Lord Harley did, indeed, possess a copy of Beckford's travel journal, and it was even more fortunate that he permitted Stephen to borrow it.

Stephen's gamble that Lady Maryann had begun her travels

out of the tiny port at Margate, as Beckford had done, paid off when a ferryman there not only remembered the beautiful blonde noblewoman but also conveyed to Stephen the information that she had hired a coach in that very city.

Like Beckford, Lady Maryann arrived on the Continent in the unremarkable Flemish seaport of Ostend. During his quest to find her, he had been able to confirm that from there she went to Ghent and from there to Antwerp. He had also been able to determine that she did not linger in any of those towns but merely passed a night in the most comfortable lodgings to be had before moving along to the next town where she intended to sleep.

Stephen's first false step occurred when he turned northward toward the Dutch cities, as Beckford had done. Nowhere in either Meerdyke, Rotterdam, or Delft could he find a soul who had seen the beautiful lone Englishwoman.

Throughout the journey Stephen had little need to flash the miniature of the lovely Lady Maryann Beresford when making his inquiries. All he had to do was to preface his inquiries with, "Have you seen a beautiful young English lady traveling alone?" and to a man, everyone remembered the lovely blonde.

Until he'd hit the brick wall in Meerdyke.

By the time he'd reached Delft and still had not found a Dutch soul who'd seen her, he knew she had not availed herself of the opportunity to see the windmills and wet lowlands of Holland. She must have headed for the Alps that would take her to Austria and to her sister.

Instead of continuing on to The Hague or Amsterdam, as had Beckford, Stephen dejectedly headed to Spa.

How many days had she gained on him now? The pity of it was that she'd had two days' start on him already. How would he be able to make up the deficit? He had the advantage of a more superior coach built by London's best carriage make. It was assured of being lighter and faster than the aged one she had hired.

He had to hope that, having never before been on the Continent, she would be so eager to see new sights she would stay in some places longer than she'd stopped at Ostend or Ghent.

He still recalled his first diplomatic mission to The Hague and how enthralled he had been to explore all the new sights from the cathedral at Ghent to castles, to the canals which striped Holland like a fine tapestry.

He was also hoping that since she was a delicate female she would not be able to tolerate as many hours in a chilly carriage as he could. His years of shooting during frigid predawn hours had inured him to a level of discomfort that few ladies could bear.

More than ten days passed before he picked up the lady's trail again in Ulm. At a half-timbered coaching inn there, the proprietor remembered Lady Maryann. In German, he told Stephen that he had been surprised to learn so fine a lady was traveling without a maid.

"How many days ago was she here?" Stephen asked.

The portly fellow pursed his lips and pondered the question a moment before answering. "I remember now. It was Sunday night."

So she was only three days ahead of him. Stephen's breakneck pace had been rewarded. By his calculations, he could catch her by the next Monday.

As maddening as the lady was—and he would throttle one of his own sisters had they dared to act like the wayward Lady Maryann—he was relieved that she was still unharmed.

At least she had been on Sunday.

One had only to look at some of these dismal inns along the way to shudder for the lady's fate. Most of them were run by dirty fellows who might slit one's throat for two pence.

Stephen hoped to God she had carried her own good locks.

And a weapon.

Though it would serve her right if she perished in one of these foreign hovels.

But since her brother had charged Stephen with her wellbeing, Stephen was committed to seeing that she reached Vienna unharmed.

It was a daunting assignment.

But Stephen prided himself on his reliability.

CHAPTER TWO

P HYSICAL MISERY ASIDE, Mary would certainly have an interesting account to tell her grandchildren about the experience of crossing these alpine footpaths. From all those travel books she'd devoured, she'd learned about the armies of men and mules it took to convey a single traveler—as well as her carriage, her trunks, and the coachmen—day after day along mountain paths too narrow and too steep for conveyances. No amount of reading, though, could have prepared her for the reality.

These mountain men most certainly did need to be such giants. Even if she was slightly built, it took a great amount of strength and stamina to carry her for hours on end, day after day—and not once stumble.

She had mounted a chair-like seat that was affixed to two poles, with one man taking the front sticks while another took the rear.

How amazing it was to watch their sure footing as they trod pathways obliterated by relentless snow, where one misstep could plunge them hundreds of feet to their deaths.

For the heavier French brothers who'd come after them, it was taking six men for each passenger because the men doing the work needed to be spelled.

When Mary's fellows needed a rest, they merely plopped her

on the ice—that's when she regretted most that her "chair" had no legs—and they would chat up with one another for a few moments. All the while, she was strapped into her legless chair on the frozen earth, quite certain she was going to perish of the cold.

What bothered Mary the most about her alpine transport, though, wasn't the lack of warming furs or the endless succession of white mountain caps or even the persistent fear of death. It was that there was no way to tuck in her dangling, icy feet.

She was in possession of the morbid fear her feet would freeze. Her daydreams consisted of pondering how she would get by once each foot had to be whacked off by an insensitive surgeon. As a double amputee, she would never be able to dance again. She'd be in Vienna and be prohibited from dancing a waltz in the city where it was born. And however would she ride? What a pity it would be to have to rely on groomsmen to hoist her footless body on top a horse! Would she have to glide through the rest of her life in a sedan chair? Even in her own house, the chair men would have to convey her up and down the stairs.

Worst of all, how could she possibly attract a husband when she was void of essential body parts? She began to feel very sorry for herself.

When she wasn't thoroughly coveting Miss Willets' huge fur boots, she daydreamed about sitting before a blazing fire, her stocking-clad feet shoved close to the flames.

On the fifth day, something occurred that superseded her fear of losing both her feet. On that day, she had good reason to truly fear for her life.

Just when she had assured herself of the steadiness of her chair men, that they were not going to slip and fall to their deaths, the very ground they were on began to shake.

Her first thought was that an earthquake had struck, but she didn't think this was the country for them.

An avalanche! Trembling with terror and certain she must be about to die, she whirled around. A mammoth blanket of white came hurling down the mountainside with the speed and power of a waterfall, ripping gargantuan conifers from the frozen earth.

She screamed. Miss Willets screamed. Her heart was beating out of her chest.

Even seeing that their group narrowly missed the avalanche's deadly path did not diminish her uncontrollable shaking, did not quell the sobs she tried to stifle.

It *was* comforting to know her life had been spared but, nevertheless, she kept thinking *I could have died*. Her nerves were rattled for the rest of that day. She could not wrench the terrifying memory from her mind.

That night, she woke up screaming. She'd awakened just as—in her dream—she was about to be buried under an avalanche.

Thereafter, no day passed that she did not worry about dying beneath a torrent of frozen earth.

As uncharacteristic as it was for her to admit to her errors, she had come to frequently lament that she had not waited until spring to commence this journey. But there you have it. Patience was a virtue Mary lacked. Which might help to explain why her embroidery resembled something executed by a demented blind person.

Prior to this trip, she had been stupid enough to believe one simply climbed a mountain and came down the other side to . . . civilization. But one mountain led to another, and then to another, and all were the same mass of endless white peaks.

Chalets she once would have disdained for their filth and austerity now became welcome beacons late each afternoon as the sun tucked itself behind another of the never-ending mountains.

During those evenings, she and Miss Willets would eat cheese and drink milk and nasty-tasting wine as they thawed in front of the fire in whichever of their tiny chambers afforded the most space.

On this, their eighth successive night crossing the mountains, there was a knock on Miss Willets' chamber door. She padded in her stockinged feet to open it, and there stood one of the French brothers who had been in their party since the beginning.

This was Pierre Fontaine, who reminded Mary of a sausage because of his short, squatty build. His brother, on the other hand, brought to mind an unscrupulous groom her father had been forced to sack. Though she doubted these men were disreputable—disreputable men would not be charged with attendance at an important event such as the Congress of Vienna as these men were—their swarthy skin, lean shabby clothing, and bad teeth most certainly resembled that scoundrel Neelys.

"Could I trouble you for the cards you so graciously offered to loan us?" Pierre Fontaine asked.

Mrs. Willets retrieved them from her valise and gave them to the grateful man.

The women had decided they preferred passing their evenings in conversation instead of playing card games.

Once she returned to her chair in front of the fire, the always-cheerful Miss Willets' brows lowered. "I fear if the snow keeps up at this rate, we may find ourselves unable to continue."

Miss Willets might be an elderly spinster, but Mary had come to value her wisdom. How did one who'd led so sheltered a life instructing young children come to know so much? By her own admission, the lady had never before been to Austria—or even to Switzerland. Yet she had acquired even more knowledge about these travels than Mary, who'd read an inordinate number of volumes on the topic.

Obviously, the governess knew more than Mary about how to dress for this frigid climate. Once more, Mary stole a jealous look at the woman's furry boots. She'd removed them in order to stick her stockinged feet in front of the fire.

Mary groaned. "I might have to fling myself from the highest peak rather than spend the winter in one of these beastly chalets. Do these people eat nothing more than cheese?" She was being flippant. The pathetic culinary offerings were perhaps the least annoying thing in her litany of discomforts at these meager inns.

Miss Willets shrugged. "There is the bread, though I will

own, they don't seem to mind whether it's fresh."

"I've begun to suspect they have an affinity for stale bread."

"You may be right, my dear."

Normally, Mary would quip back that she was always right, but this journey had all but destroyed her confidence. She sighed. "Do you really think there's a likelihood we could be stranded in these mountains for weeks on end?"

"It happens."

Did the woman have to be so pragmatic? Mary groaned again. "I thought by leaving England in November and by forfeiting the opportunity to see Holland and castles and many lures of the Continent, I'd be able to cross the mountains before winter set in."

"And you should have." The older woman sighed. "Such a pity that seasons cannot read calendars. Sometimes they come before they're supposed to."

"The only thing worse than being forced to spend winter here would be to be forced to spend it here without you."

The older lady's pink face brightened. "I feel just as fortunate to have you as a companion on my travels."

"But you make me feel beastly inadequate. How did you know you needed such wonderful boots?"

"Try them on, dear one. It has not escaped my notice how much you admire them."

Mary's feet fit neatly into the boots. Fur was inside as well as out. "They feel divine. How is it you managed to procure them in France?"

"While the family for whom I was employed did live in Paris, they also had a chateau in the mountains. I'm sure you would never have heard of the village where it was located for there can't be as many as thirty inhabitants. We went there twice a year. The children loved the snow. One of the local farmers there spent his winters fashioning the most wonderful items from furs, and my employers saw to it that everyone in their household possessed boots made by the aged farmer. Unfortunately, the farmer's dead now, but I'm very happy to have his boots. I daresay they'll outlast me."

"Did you say your new employer is in Vienna with the diplomatic corps for the Congress?"

"Yes. He's some kind of an important French official, but I'm vastly ignorant about matters of government. Is your sister's husband in government?"

"No. He's involved with banking. You may have heard of his family. They're Birminghams."

Miss Willets' eyes widened. "Though I've been gone from England for many years, I had heard that a Birmingham was said to be the richest man in England."

Mary nodded. "That was probably Will's father." Mary nodded. "They are obscenely wealthy—but you'd never know it. They're neither arrogant nor ostentatious. There are three brothers, and their sister's wed to Lord Agar. You'd never find a more gracious lady."

Miss Willets' yawns grew more frequent. Mary finally stood. "My bed—such that it is—beckons." She patted Miss Willet's shoulders.

"Try not to worry, my lady," Mrs. Willets said in a soothing voice. "Hopefully, the weather will clear tomorrow."

STEPHEN HAD A stroke of luck at the bank where he'd gone to exchange his letter of credit for Swiss currency. The clerk there remembered the beautiful young English noblewoman, and when Stephen produced her miniature, he confirmed it.

Fortuitously, the lady had requested from the bank clerk a recommendation for her transport across the mountains, and Stephen went to the same establishment. That assured him he would be taking the same route across the mountains as she had.

As happy as he was that he'd closed the gap between them by

two days, she was still one day ahead of him. And there'd be no way now for him to make up any more time. There were only a few hours of daylight—at this time of year less than eight—and no way to extend the day. It would be impossible to travel these mountain paths in the dark.

It pained him that he hadn't been able to catch her before the lengthy journey across the mountains. His only consolation was that if something—possibly a danger—prohibited her from continuing, he would be there for her.

Not for her as much as for Devere. He sympathized with the poor fellow. He kept thinking of his youngest sister and how fearful he would be for her safety were she to be traveling alone in a foreign land. Not that Sarah would ever contemplate anything so foolhardy.

Hadn't Devere said his sister was small? A petite young woman with large amounts of money and no man to protect her was a woman begging to be accosted. Or even worse. Stephen trembled for Devere.

He was too out of charity with the lady to have any empathy for her. He wasn't even sure he could be civil to her when he did at last meet her. The lady was in want of a brain.

The group in which he was traveling consisted of just two parties: him and two Belgian men who had not previously been acquainted. One of them—Monsieur Blanchard—was also traveling to the Congress in Vienna. The other Belgian was traveling to Munich to teach French to the children of a wealthy German family.

Because the Belgians were smaller than Stephen, they only required four chair men, who took turns carrying them up and down the winding alpine paths.

Stephen was so much larger, carrying him required six men—and cost him considerably more.

During the evenings at the chalets where they stopped for the night, Stephen had chosen not to pass the time with the Belgians. He'd spent his time reading over documents to prepare for his duties at the Congress. But on the eighth night, he accepted Blanchard's invitation to play cribbage.

"Have you visited Paris?" Stephen asked. "My father spent some time there during his Grand Tour—before the Revolution—and preferred it above all other places."

"As well he should. It is the world's greatest city, and—whether you admire the late emperor or not—you would have to agree that the capital's architecture under his reign is unquestionably the most beautiful in all of Europe."

"I look forward to seeing it—and Vienna. I've not been there before. Have you?" Stephen asked.

"This will also be my first visit there."

Stephen wondered why Blanchard would be coming to Vienna from the lowlands instead of the usual route from France. It was certainly not Stephen's business to ask personal questions.

They played cribbage until nearly midnight. Stephen had to admit after all these solitary weeks of travel, it was good to have interaction with someone else—even though the two were so engaged in their respective games, they spoke little.

Travel the following day was the worst yet. Snow fell from the moment they started until dusk set upon them. He nearly despaired that they'd be stranded to die on a white mountaintop with no shelter for as far as they could see.

When the chair men were lumbering through snow up to their knees, and seeing twenty feet ahead was difficult, they rounded a mountain peak and on the descent far below the indistinct yellow glow from what must be lighted windows was perhaps the most welcome sight he'd ever seen.

When they reached the valley he was pleased to see the largest chalet they'd yet encountered. The surrounding outbuildings consisted of a barn, a stable, and an assortment of cottages all hugging close to the three-story chalet.

He didn't know it yet, but he was about to meet Lady Maryann Beresford. Or, as she now called herself, Lady Mary Beresford.

CHAPTER THREE

M ARY HAD READ about altitude sickness. She'd even feared it because she was cursed with a devilishly overactive stomach. She'd thought that since she had traipsed for eight days through these mountains with no ill effects, she had been spared The Curse.

Then on the ninth day—a miserable, brutally cold day in which she feared they were about to encounter a blizzard—her stomach betrayed her.

She didn't think anything could be worse than the channel crossing. At one point while her boat—at least that's what she called it—was bobbing on the seas as if it were a cork, she fleetingly thought dying would be a welcome relief from having to endure another nauseating moment aboard the wretched vessel.

Today was worse. Each careful step of her chair men swished the contents of her stomach. In spite of the cold, her face grew hot. The very memory of the previous night's cheese could invoke a . . . spewing.

So in addition to her physical misery, she was humiliated at the trail she was leaving behind. Her chair men were awfully kind about it all. They assured her they were accustomed to such passengers. "It is very common," they told her in their curious tongue, which she had no trouble understanding. Nevertheless, she was embarrassed.

And she pitied those who came after her.

When she got her first glimpse of the valley where they would spend the night, she could have gotten down on her knees and prayed her thanks.

She allowed herself to hope it would be as inviting on the inside as it appeared from a distance. In style, the inn was the typical Tyrolean timbered house with sharp gables and smoke curling from the chimneys. But unlike the previous inns where they had stayed, this one was considerably larger—three main stories plus a dormered garret. A dozen chimneys jutted from the steeply sloped roof. Several outbuildings nestled around the main house.

Weak and so nauseous it was difficult for her to walk or talk, she rushed to her chamber and—snatching the chamber pot to place beside her—climbed atop the tall feather bed. She was too sick to even put her own linens on the bed.

That night, she slept like the dead.

When she awakened the following morning, she was dismayed to realize she had slept in her clothing. All previous notions of fashionable dress had been disavowed during this trying journey. For today, she would merely cover her wrinkled clothing with a voluminous shawl. Then, of course, when they left the chalet, she would don her heavy velvet cloak. No one would notice how wrinkled her dress was.

Surprisingly, her chamber wasn't too cold. Her fire had gone out, but smoldering embers still gave off a little heat. She crossed the wooden floor to lift the homespun curtains and peer from the window. She hadn't remembered she was on the third floor, but being up that high offered a good view of the surrounding buildings.

How could the sun be shining when snow was falling so hard? Deep snowdrifts, she was sure, would prohibit the opening of the barn door directly across from her room.

She vaguely recalled being told this inn offered an eating

room. She wasn't confident enough in her stomach to eat, but she would enjoy a cup of steaming tea and a chat with Miss Willets, who was sure to have missed her last night.

Taking her tea tin with her, Mary went down two flights of stairs and followed the voices to the eating room. It was a large chamber with one wall centered by a rock fireplace where a fire roared. A scattering of tables could seat more than twenty people. Behind this chamber was a another for servants. She recognized her coachman seated there.

Miss Willets must have slept late, for she wasn't in the eating room. Mary selected a table close to the fire and soon told the attendant she didn't need food but would like a pot of hot water for her tea. Hopefully, her stomach would be able to tolerate a wee bit of cream.

She was embarrassed to see the French brothers who came behind them each day. They had to have seen the evidence of her illness splattering the snow the previous day. She took a seat on the opposite side of the fireplace from where the three of them sat, her chair not facing the men.

Curiously, the chamber was being shared by a couple she'd not seen before. She knew enough Italian to determine they were speaking in that language, and she determined they must be husband and wife. She would guess them to be in their forties. Both were possessed of dark hair. The man's manner of dress indicated a level of affluence. It was difficult to tell about the woman's clothing for it was covered by a voluminous knitted shawl. Mary herself eschewed those shawls in favor of the finer ones from Kashmir.

Mary had to own it was good to see another female. She peered at the woman's feet. No fur boots, but leather ones— much more practical than Mary's meager half boots that barely came to her ankle.

When Mary finished her tea and Miss Willets still hadn't come, she became alarmed. The woman was not young. Perhaps she had taken ill. This was an exceedingly rigorous journey.

Mary had best check on her.

She wandered around the ground floor until she found a man who looked vaguely familiar. Was he the one who'd shown her to her chamber yesterday?

"Good morning, Lady Mary," said the man with the proprietary air. He looked to be the same age as Miss Willets. Even his bushy gray eyebrows and hair were the same color as hers.

"Could you tell me which room Miss Willets is in?"

His brows lowered. "But there is no Miss Willets staying at Le Chateau."

How was it the man could remember Mary's name and have no knowledge of Miss Willets? Had the lady used another name? "The older lady." Mary's hand indicated a height less than her own. "Her hair is silver, and she wears spectacles."

He shook his head. "There's no such person here."

"Of course there is. She was just in front of me."

"My lady, you were quite ill when you arrived. Perhaps your mind is confused."

She bristled. "There's nothing the matter with my mind."

"Do forgive me. It's just that you were . . . disoriented when you came here yesterday evening."

He was right—about her being disoriented, not about poor Miss Willets. "I do believe you are mistaken."

Then it occurred to Mary that she was so sick on arrival, perhaps she had slept for four-and-twenty hours. Perhaps Miss Willets had left yesterday. She would have asked this man what day it was, but Mary had lost track of the days. She couldn't have said if it was Thursday or Sunday. And she certainly did not want him to think her any more *disoriented* than he already thought her.

She stormed back to the eating room and up to the table where the pair of Frenchmen sat. "Pardon me for disturbing you, but have you seen the little lady who was traveling just ahead of me, the one with silver hair and spectacles?" These men had been in their group since the first day—which she believed to be ten days ago.

Brows lifted, they looked at one another, shaking their heads.

So they hadn't seen her this morning. "Would you know which room she was assigned?"

Charles Fontaine responded. "We've not seen any silver-haired lady."

"She's the one who loaned you a deck of cards a few nights ago."

They looked at one another and continued to shake their heads. The Fontaine brother she suspected to be the youngest answered this time. "We never borrowed cards from anyone. We've never seen such a lady as you describe."

A stinging rage coursed through her. How could the despicable man so brazenly lie?

The other brother spoke. "Mademoiselle was very sick yesterday. It will take time for you to recover all your faculties."

Anger consumed her as powerfully as yesterday's nausea. "I am in possession of all my faculties." Giving them The Glare, she turned and left.

How could it be she was the only one here who had *not* taken leave of her senses? Why were all of them conspiring against her to deny the existence of Miss Willets?

She must find Miss Willets' chair men. Once again, she came to the authoritative man with the bushy gray hair. It was impossible for her to speak to him without betraying her rancor. "Where can I find the chair men?"

"They are staying in the cottage next to the barn, but I believe they are already packing the mules for today's journey."

She went back upstairs to put on her cloak and heavy gloves to brave the cold. At each chamber door she passed, she hoped to get a glimpse of Miss Willets. She would show them!

But not a single door opened.

As she was coming back down the stairs, one of the chair men—hers, actually—was coming up. "I shall get my lady's valise now," he told her.

The valise was the last thing they packed each morning.

"Do you know where I can find the older lady with silver hair and spectacles?"

His brows lowered. "I am afraid I don't know any such lady."

Perhaps the fellow only paid attention to the woman who was in his care. His youth—since he was likely younger than she—would explain why he would not have paid attention to a meek little silver-haired old lady. "Well, please tell me where I can find the pair of chair men who journeyed right in front us each day."

He gave her a quizzing look. "But, my lady, we were the first ones each day, and the only others in our group were the Frenchmen who traveled behind us."

His words were like the plunge of a saber. Everyone was against her. She wanted to scream. She wanted to slap him. "Why are you lying to me?"

"But, my lady, I am not. You have been sick. Perhaps your distress has . . . confused you."

She stomped her foot. "I. Am. Not. Confused."

"Forgive me." His tone lightened. "We are about to leave. I see you are ready."

"I'm not leaving without Miss Willets!"

"But you must leave."

"I am the one who's paying you. You're to do as I request, and I say I'm not leaving at this time."

"But, my lady . . ."

Her eyes narrowed. "My decision is inflexible."

She went back to her bedchamber. She wasn't sure what she was going to do or how she was going to find Miss Willets, but she could not ignore that sweet lady's absence. She meant to find out why there was a conspiracy to deny Miss Willets' existence.

AT THE END of this freezing, miserably uncomfortable day he'd thought would never end, the large chalet was indeed a welcome sight. This had been the worst day yet, and the snowstorm gave no signs of abating. What rotten luck it would be to get stranded there while Lady Mary gained on him by several days. She might even—provided she did not encounter danger—reach Vienna without his assistance. For Devere's sake, Stephen hoped she would stay safe.

But he had serious doubts.

His expectations of the lodgings were more than fulfilled. Le Chateau, as the inn was called, was by far the largest one in which they had stayed. It even had an eating room, which was a welcome change from munching on cheese and stale bread in his meager bedchambers that did not even provide a table. He was so hungry, the prospect of munching on cheese and stale bread even appealed.

This journey was the first time in his life he had not dressed for dinner. He merely went to his assigned third-floor chamber, shed his outer garments, and came back downstairs to the eating room. Humphrey would be livid. Stephen's valet took it as a personal affront when his master did not dress to perfection— especially for dinner.

Upon entering the chamber, he almost stood still to stare at what he saw. To his astonishment, there at a table all by herself sat Lady Mary Beresford. He could not reveal his interest. At least not now. Devere had asked him not to. He continued on to the table next to her and situated himself so that he could look at the young woman.

Her miniature did not do her justice. He'd known she was lovely but, in the flesh, she was even more beautiful. In spite of her exposure to frost and winds, her skin was as pure as a bowl of fresh cream. Each feature, from her perfect nose to her large blue eyes, feathered together flawlessly. Her blonde locks had been carelessly swept back in the Grecian mode.

That she dressed tastefully in a pale blue velvet gown did not surprise him. The Beresfords were noted for their impeccable fashion sense. His gaze lazily swept over her body. Most young women as delicately built as she resembled young boys. But not her. She curved in the appropriate places.

The lady was perfection.

A pity she was in want of sense.

She also appeared to be in a state of deep melancholy. Instead of the tweak of a playful smile he'd detected in her portrait, her face was now marked by sorrow. It was no wonder. The trip was wretchedly wearing on one and, by now, she must be regretting her decision to travel—and to travel alone.

He noticed she was eating some kind of meat. Thank God. He hadn't had meat since Ulm. Whether it be rabbit or beef, he would greedily consume it. Soon, a flaxen-haired serving girl delivered his plate, and he dug in appreciatively.

He told himself he needed to befriend the lady. But he would not reveal that he knew Devere, nor would he tell her he'd been following her. Other than that, he would be truthful, would use his real name, and would explain his mission in Vienna.

After she finished eating, she went to get up.

He stood, eyeing her. "Pardon my boldness, but you appear to be a fellow countryman of mine."

A huge smile brightened her already extraordinary face. "You're English!" She sounded as he imagined Robinson Crusoe might have after his decades without encountering another white man.

"Indeed I am. If I might be so bold, allow me to introduce myself." He offered a courtly bow. "Lord Stephen Stanhope, at your service, miss." He did not want to reveal he knew she was addressed as *my lady*.

She dipped into a curtsy. "Lady Mary Beresford." She pursed her lips. "You are the son of the Duke of Lancaster?"

"I am. Fourth son, so no dukedom in my future, I'm afraid," he said with a smile. He did not like to lie, but thought it expedient to do so at this time—not that he would actually be lying.

He would merely omit telling her he was acquainted with her brother. He *had* been slightly acquainted with her older sister. "Beresford? Let me see, I did know a Lady Sophia Beresford."

"My sister. I'm traveling to see her in Vienna."

"That happens to be where I am going."

"Are you attached to the Foreign Office?"

He nodded. "Have been since the day I left Oxford."

She flashed an angry glance at a pair of men he'd heard speaking in French. "I can't tell you how comforting it is to finally have the company of an Englishman."

The way she'd looked at the Frenchmen made him wonder if they had harmed her in some way. "It's far too early to go to bed. Would you permit me to further our conversation at the inglenook?" He had noticed the comforting little fire-lit alcove next to this room.

"But you haven't finished your dinner."

He smiled. "I devoured my meat, and that's all that matters." He stepped closer to her and offered his crooked arm. "It's no great sacrifice to leave the stale bread."

She linked her arm to his, and they went to the inglenook and sat next to each other on one of a pair of smooth wooden benches that flanked the rock fireplace.

"Tell me, my lady, how it is that your party is here this evening when you've not been in front of us at any time during the journey? Surely the snow isn't so bad that you cannot progress. Has someone in your group taken ill?"

She gazed at the roaring fire and did not answer him for a moment. "It's my fault our party has not progressed."

"You have been ill?"

Again, she hesitated before responding. "I was ill the day before yesterday."

"You appear to have recovered."

"Yes," she said in a forlorn voice. "Two days ago, I suffered from an acute case of altitude sickness. It was even worse than the sickness that gripped me during the channel crossing."

So the lady was possessed of what his mother referred to as a weak stomach. "That can make one dangerously ill, I've been told."

"If you haven't experienced it, it's difficult to understand just how debilitating it can be." She took a deep breath. "When we arrived here I was too ill to communicate. I went straight to my chamber and flung myself on the bed. Now they're all against me."

His brows lowered with concern. "Who's against you?"

"Everyone."

Devere had said his sister was possessed of a dramatic flair. "You're saying everyone is against you because you were sick?"

A frustrated look on her face, she shook her head. "They're all lying."

"About what?"

"About Miss Willets."

Was he supposed to know who Miss Willets was? "Who is Miss Willets?"

"She's a little old English governess who was traveling with me. She was on her way to start employment for the family of a French diplomat in Vienna."

"She has turned the others against you?"

She shook her head. "No, not that. She's a lovely person. It's the others. Everyone here—including my own chair men—deny her existence. Miss Willets has completely disappeared."

He could not help but remember Devere saying his sister did not always speak truthfully. "You're saying she started the journey with you?"

"Yes. She was just in front of me throughout the entire trip. And because we were both English, we befriended one another. We'd meet each night in our rooms."

This was a most peculiar tale. "What of her chair men?"

"They're gone, too. And my chair men are now lying about Miss Willets' existence, too."

The lady must be delusional. "How does this explain why you did not continue on your journey today?"

"How could I? Miss Willets might need my help. I cannot abandon her."

"But how could you be abandoning her if she's not here?"

"She must be here, or someone here must know where she is. I refuse to go on until I find out."

"Why are the others staying?"

"Because I would not leave, none in my party could go. Now, the Frenchmen are furious with me because they claim I'm impeding their progress. But they're horrid men."

His brows lowered. "They've harmed you?"

"Only by their lies."

"What kind of lies?"

"When I asked them to confirm that Miss Willets was traveling with us, they lied. They even lied about her lending them a deck of cards."

"You're saying they claim she did not exist?"

"Exactly."

This was a strange story, to be sure. "What does all of this have to do with your illness?"

She shrugged. "Because I was so sick upon coming here, they say I was disoriented, that my mind is confused. They're trying to tell me I'm delusional, that I made her up."

"Who's saying this?"

"Everyone. The Frenchmen. My chair men. The gray-haired man who must be the proprietor. All of them say Miss Willets was conjured by my imagination during my sickness."

He had never heard of a nausea sickness affecting one's mind, but there was a significant imbalance of opinion as to the veracity of the old lady's existence. Lady Mary was the only one of . . . seven different people who denied Miss Willets, and only one claimed to have seen her. This was a most baffling account.

Lady Mary must be a most peculiar woman. Yet Stephen had given his word he would protect her. He supposed that meant protecting her against those here who mistreated her. Even if she was, indeed, delusional. "So you refused to leave this morning. What did you do today?"

"I looked around, trying to find Miss Willets."

The poor lady could not own up to her wild imagination. He decided to humor her. "Where did you look?"

"In the barn. In the stables. I wanted to look in all the rooms here, but that wretched proprietor forbade me. He said all the rooms are occupied, and I had no right to disturb his guests. He's lying, of course."

"What, precisely, is he lying about—other than Miss Willets?"

"About every chamber being occupied. I counted heads, and I've counted doors. There is a great disparity. Miss Willets must be in one of those room." Her lashes lowered. "Or else they've killed her."

Her mental imbalance was almost laughable. "Come now, why would all these perfect strangers be conspiring to kill a harmless old lady?"

She shook her head. "I have thought and thought about it, but I just don't know."

None of it made any sense. Why in the devil had he allowed himself to be sucked into this situation?

Lady Mary needed to forget all this nonsense and continue on the journey. And he meant to see to it that she did. "Will you leave tomorrow, then?"

"Of course not! I can't. I'm worried about Miss Willets. Something's happened to her, and I mean to find out what." She looked up at him, tears pooling in those spectacular pale blue eyes. "Will you please help me?"

He was perplexed. Was this woman lying? He had given Devere his word he'd help his sister. Once again, he thought of Sarah. If his sister were so far from home, alone, he hoped someone would help her. "I'll help."

He would help disprove her Miss Willets.

Chapter Four

WHAT A PECULIAR predicament she was in to be rejoicing that a blizzard would prevent her party from continuing on the journey. As had become her custom, the first thing Mary did upon awakening was to pad over to her chamber window and observe the landscape. Normally, it did not vary. Today it did.

She had known from the intensity of the storm that woke her several times throughout the night that it was something out of the ordinary, but she was unprepared for the snowdrifts that came more than halfway up the first floor of the inn. As she watched from her window, she realized it would be impossible for the chair men and mules to move through snow this deep. Nor would she want them to—if she had not already resolved to stay here until she located Miss Willets.

These odious inhabitants of Le Chateau would not be able to blame her today for being stranded here, though she supposed they still would. Had she not impeded their progress yesterday, they could possibly have outdistanced this storm.

Those horrid people would continue to loathe her—which she did not resent in the least, seeing that she despised them. Liars all.

All except for Lord Stephen. She was so gratified to have an ally. And what an ally he was! Not only was he compassionate toward her—a quality she dearly needed right now—but he was also a fine-looking man.

Even at a London ball, he would have stood out from all the insipid men who paid her court. It wasn't just his thick, dark hair and admirable height that would have distinguished him. Nor his broad shoulders and muscled legs that filled out a pair of breeches. His handsome face was more than physically pleasing. In it, there was maturity, character, strength—and he was possessed of a kindly smile. When those near-black eyes of his regarded her, she experienced the oddest sensation that her breath thinned—and not from the altitude.

Had Lord Stephen not been attached to the diplomatic corps and traipsing about the Continent these past several years, he most certainly would have been snatched up by a beautiful London debutante of noble birth, as befit his rank as the son of a duke.

Today, she would dress carefully to look her best when she went down to the eating room. Not for the first time, she lamented she hadn't brought her maid.

Once she was as satisfied as she could be with her appearance, under the circumstances, she went directly to the eating room, sweeping past that disgusting proprietor without even attempting a greeting.

She wasn't sure if she should sit with Lord Stephen, but he took the decision from her hands when he rose upon her entrance to the chamber. "I beg that you join me, Lady Mary."

She favored him with a smile and came to sit beside him, noting that the chamber was already occupied by the French brothers and two other males, and the Italian couple. Why the Italians had remained, where they had come from, and what route they were taking all aroused questions in Mary's mind.

"Since I refuse to speak to any of these beasts, you must inform me of what is going on," she said.

Lord Stephen's face broke into a grin. What fine white teeth he possessed. "There's no telling how long we'll be forced to stay here since a blizzard came through during the night, dumping more than four feet of snow, and the snow's not relenting." He sighed. "And I don't need to tell you that you're as popular with your fellow guests as Napoleon is with the English."

"And I have no more love for them. They're appallingly untruthful. And that's putting it far more kindly than they deserve!"

"At least if we have to be stuck somewhere, you must own this is easily the most comfortable inn we've encountered since leaving the foothills."

"Yes, quite."

"Mr. Becker has every right to be proud of his Le Chateau."

Her eyes narrowed. "So that's the name of that wicked man with the wild gray hair?"

He grinned. "It is."

A plump young woman with thick blonde braids delivered Mary's plate with mounds of freshly churned butter, a slab of bread, and some kind of soft cheese, which Mary reluctantly admitted tasted even better than her favorite English cheese. This was accompanied by a glass of chilled milk.

Clutching her tea tin, Mary requested a cup of boiling water. She noticed Lord Stephen, too, had brought his own tea.

"I am surprised, Lady Mary, that your family has permitted you to travel alone like this."

"Oh, they didn't permit it." She gazed up at him. "I am one-and-twenty. I no longer need my brother's permission."

"Your brother must be mad with worry. Do you not expect him to be hurrying after you?"

She shrugged. "I do feel bad if I've caused him any consternation, but he won't be able to come after me. You see, my poor brother suffered a badly broken leg and must keep it elevated."

"Then I feel compelled to look after you as your brother would have done."

She was incredibly touched by his kindness toward her, but the idea of thinking of Lord Stephen as a brother was laughable. She could never feel sisterly toward a man as appealing as him.

"You are very kind."

The girl brought their hot water, and Mary busied herself preparing her tea, buttering her bread, and sampling both.

"So," he said, "do we act as if we've long known each other, or do we own up to the truth—that we've only just met?"

She pondered his question for a moment. "Speaking only for myself, I should like it to appear that I've an ally. It's wretched when everyone is against you."

"Then I shall be your old friend," he said with a smile.

"There is the fact, too, you're the largest man here."

"What does that have to do with anything?"

"It will be more difficult for those terrible men to bully me."

"They've bullied you?"

"Certainly. They've dismissed everything I had to say by brushing it off as coming from a woman who's clearly mentally incompetent. Let them do that now that I have . . . a champion." Her voice dropped at that last word. "At least I hope I do?"

His hand covered hers, and her heart lifted. "I will be your advocate," he said.

"I don't think this is the best place for us to discuss this conspiracy."

"We cannot always be guaranteed of having the inglenook to ourselves."

"As much as these people detest me, I believe we can. If we get there first, no others will want to sit there with us. To them, I'm as bad as a leper." Her gaze fanned over the chamber, and then her voice dropped. "Have you noticed the Italian couple?"

He went to look at them, and she swatted his hand. "Don't look now! I merely wished to point them out because they're quite suspicious."

"In what way?" he asked in a whisper as he poured some of his milk into his tea.

"They were here my first morning, and where they came from I couldn't say. They were neither in front of us nor behind us."

x

"Can you tell if they're going or coming to Italy?"

She shrugged. "I have no idea. I don't even know if Italy is their destination or their point of embarkation."

"Perhaps they, too, are on the way to Vienna."

"They're utterly suspicious. Why, for example, did they continue to stay here yesterday after my group was prohibited from advancing because I refused to go on without Miss Willets?"

He sighed. "We'd best save this discussion. So . . . did your maid accompany you?"

"I shall be flattered by your question."

"How so?"

"Because it must not be obvious that I—who am devoid of any kind of talent—have styled my hair myself."

He tossed back his head and laughed. "Your hair is lovely."

"The first thing I shall do when I reach Vienna will be to procure a maid. I had no notion that dressing oneself could be so difficult. Did your valet come with you?"

"He did. Do I look agreeable?"

He was most decidedly swoon-worthy. "Indeed you do. Now I shall feel shabby."

"You look lovely."

"Of course you would say that. You're a career diplomat. You're accustomed to flattery."

"I am not flattering you."

They chatted for a few moments about mutual acquaintances, then she broached the subject of his travels. "Have you ever been to Vienna before?"

He shook his head. "I haven't traveled as much as others attached to the Foreign Office, probably owing to the many years Napoleon's controlled so much of Europe. I spent three years at The Hague, but most of my service has been at Whitehall."

"Then I'm all the more shocked we haven't encountered one another."

"Since my duties require me to be in London, I take every opportunity I can to be in the country. I enjoy shooting at

Pangburn Abbey, a place I prefer over all others."

"When in London, do you never go to Almack's?"

He gave a mock shudder. "Heavens no! Is that not where one goes when one wishes to be besieged by mothers foisting their plain daughters upon matrimonial prospects?"

She giggled. "You have aptly described it."

"But nevertheless you go there?"

"On occasion."

"That you are one-and-twenty and still unwed while also being beautiful tells me none of the men there suited you. You must be like your sister. I know as fact Lady Sophia turned down dozens of offers."

Mary was still almost levitational over him calling her beautiful. "That's true. She set a good example for me. Her long wait certainly paid off for she ended up with a man possessed of every quality one could wish for in a husband."

"The man was most fortunate to have won Lady Sophia's hand."

Their plates were cleaned, and their tea was drunk. None of the others had yet left. What else was there to do in the monotonous hours that stretched before them but to sit around and talk?

Well, those lying Frenchmen could play with Miss Willets' cards—but, of course, they wouldn't for fear of having to confess their lies. Just thinking of them denying Miss Willets and her cards made Mary's temper flare.

"Come," she said. "Let's go to the inglenook before one of them claims it."

He rose. "A good idea."

THE ONLY REASON he had agreed to go along with her desire to act as if they were old friends was his desire to protect her from the others' wrath—not that she didn't deserve it but, nevertheless, she elicited sympathy in him.

As pretty as he'd thought her last evening, he found her even prettier today. She not only looked well rested, but everything about her looked fresh. She wore a fetching pale canary yellow dress that made her look as delicate as a woodland flower.

"Now, my lady," he began, "have you thought of any reason why anyone would wish to either abduct or . . . or harm your elderly traveling companion?" *If there was such a companion.*

He had a difficult time believing Lady Mary's story when seven others refuted it. And when her own brother had warned that she was not always truthful.

But Stephen had to admit, she sounded convincing, so convincing he found himself wondering if she was mentally impaired, as the others accused.

"Miss Willets couldn't have an enemy in the world!" Lady Mary shook her head. "She's an elderly woman who's spent her adult life imparting knowledge to young children."

"Think, my lady. What else do you know about her?" He could not help but to wonder if Lady Mary was making up the governess. What facts would she invent?

She puckered her lips in thought. "She knew my father when he was young. Her father tutored in Oxford—where she spent her early years."

He nodded. "What of her employers?"

"She said she's been away from England for many years, that she worked for a wealthy French family for many years, but I'm guessing not for, like, forty years, which is what I estimate to be the duration of years in which she's served as a governess."

"The last family who employed her . . . did she say they were wealthy?"

"She didn't actually. She said that in addition to their home in Paris they had a chateau in a small village in the French Alps, and are chateaus not always resided in by the very rich?"

"I will own they are much larger than a *maison*, so they likely were very wealthy. Did she tell you the family's name?"

Lady Mary shook her head.

"But, I take it, this is not the family she was . . . is traveling to be with in Vienna?"

"Correct. She said her other children had outgrown the need for a governess." Lady Mary made a sad face. "Our old governess is now with Lord Aynsley's family in Shropshire."

"That's all well and good, but what can you tell me about Miss Willets' new employer?"

"You're mocking me."

"I'm not mocking you. You're the one who jumped to an unrelated subject."

She pouted. "It was too related. We were talking about governess' charges growing up, and I merely spoke about our dear former governess."

"We were supposed to be confining our remarks to Miss Willets." *If there was a Miss Willets.* "I asked you to tell me what you can about her new employer."

Her eyes narrowed with disdain, she presented the impression of one deep in thought. "His family had gone to Vienna for the Congress. She said he was a very important man."

This might give him something factual with which to prove or disprove her story. "And what was . . . is his name?"

She closed her eyes as would one in deep thought. Then she shrugged. "She may have said, but I cannot remember."

Just as he feared. "How old would you estimate Miss Willets to be?"

"I'm not terribly good at aging old people. One with silver hair is much the same as another with gray hair. Except for my mother. She turned gray when she was but five-and-thirty, and she was still very beautiful. She was also blessed, I think, that powdered hair was in fashion, so most women looked to have gray hair."

He scowled and cleared his throat.

"Oh, dear, I've done it again," she said apologetically. "I've redirected your topic. You're going to be out of charity with me."

"It's not as if we don't have all day. Pray, my lady continue."

Her brows drew together. "What was your last question?"

"How old do you think Miss Willets was?"

"I would hazard to guess her age to be sixty. There. Did I give a satisfactory answer?"

"This is not a quiz."

She pouted again. "You don't have to be such a curmudgeon."

"I'm not a curmudgeon. I've never once been accused of being a curmudgeon."

"Now look who's being defensive."

"I'm not defensive. I'm merely stating a fact."

She folded her arms in front of her. "Do go ahead. We have all day."

What a maddening woman! "You cannot think of any reason why anyone would wish her harm? Did she ever mention having enemies?"

She gave him an are-you-out-of-your-mind look. "We're talking about a very small, very meek elderly woman."

Exactly. The idea of her having enemies was ludicrous. Lady Mary had to have invented her. "Then, for the sake of humoring me, try to imagine a scenario in which the woman would be threatened. Imagine, if you will, you are a gothic novelist. What precursors would put the lady in peril?"

A slow smile eased across her remarkable face, lifting the corners of her full mouth. It was a moment before she responded. "What if the lady were of noble birth and had been snatched from the cradle? Now she's in line to become queen of . . . one of those German-speaking principalities—though she doesn't know it—and she stands in the way of another inheriting. The pretender to the throne sends out her assassins to murder Miss Willets—who's actually the Princess of Plentitude." She looked up at him, beaming. "How was that?"

He nodded. He could easily see why her brother said she was given to embellishing the truth. "Interesting theory."

"That would make those dreadful Frenchmen who were following us assassins."

"Too obvious. My money's on the Italian couple. Tell me again what you know of them."

"Next to nothing. It's very suspicious they have not left the inn."

"I suppose it's not out of the question that some people would come here for a holiday."

"But there's nothing to do."

"There is that."

"From his dress, I would say they're wealthy, but I can't properly tell because her clothing is always covered with colorful knitted shawls."

"You would know better than I about fashion."

She squinted. "There is something odd . . ."

"What?"

"The woman looks at her husband as if she worships him."

"What's odd about that?"

"She's forty if she's a day. Therefore, one might assume they've been married a decade or two." She put hands to hips and stared at him. "How many long-married women do you know who ogle their husbands?"

"It's not a matter to which I've ever given consideration." He shrugged. "There is the fact they're Italians. Are Italians not more . . . amorous than our countrymen?"

"I wouldn't know, having never known an Italian. But I have heard they are noted for their grand passions to those with whom they are *not* married."

"Then perhaps our couple is having a romantic tryst. They would certainly have no need to worry about meeting acquaintances here, acquaintances who might know the other's spouse."

Her eyes flashed with mirth. "Well aren't you the devious one!"

"I am not devious."

"Of course you're not. In fact, I'm certain you were going to tell me no one has ever accused you of being devious."

"You're being contrary to the only person who's trying to help you."

"Forgive me." She did not sound contrite.

"I believe you need to befriend the lady. What could be more natural than that you'd wish to communicate with another of your gender, given the length of our confinement?"

"Perhaps you're right. And you, my dear Lord Stephen, who will you befriend?"

"Our innkeeper."

CHAPTER FIVE

H ANGING ABOUT IN one's room was far too dreary. How grateful Mary was that she'd brought books, many books, with her though she'd felt wretchedly sorry for the poor porters who had to lug her portmanteau up and down the mountains.

The inglenook was a fine spot in which to read. Not only was it comfortable, but its situation between Mr. Becker's area and the eating room also gave her the opportunity to observe the comings and goings of the other guests. Surely none of them would care to spend their days in their solitary rooms.

When she approached the inglenook, she was disappointed she would not have it to herself. The Italian couple had gotten there first. "Bonjour," she said to them, smiling as she sat on the bench opposite them.

The couple, holding hands, smiled and nodded at her. A pity she could not speak Italian. But was French not the universal language of Europe? They were bound to be able to communicate in French. "How are you?" she asked in French.

The man shrugged and responded in Italian.

Which she did not understand.

So much for befriending them. She picked up her book and began to read.

Soon, the Italians got up to leave. She smiled and nodded at them, and they reciprocated.

It was difficult for her to concentrate because intermittent laughter kept erupting from the eating room. She'd recognized the voices of the French brothers and the Belgians who'd traveled with Lord Stephen. Whatever were they doing?

She set down her book and tiptoed to the doorway of the eating room to peek in. The Frenchmen in her party had joined the Belgians from Lord Stephen's party to make a foursome for a game of whist—at least she thought it was whist. She peered closely at the cards to see if they were the same ones Miss Willets had loaned to their fellow travelers, but they were not. These had a harlequin pattern on their backs. Miss Willets' had been pastel drawings of birds.

She returned to her spot close to the blazing fire and continued reading. No more travel journals for her. All of them had been written by men. Not one had suggested furry boots. She would show them! Whenever she returned from her travels she would write her own account. She would title it *Lady Mary Beresford's Guide to Continental Travel*. It would most certainly feature helpful advice for female travelers.

Why must she wait until she returned? She ought to be writing down everything she witnessed during this journey. She flung down her book and raced back to her bedchamber to fetch the little leather-bound journal she'd started writing in at the beginning of her journey but which she had neglected lately.

When she opened her portmanteau and began rifling through her books, she was possessed by an odd feeling that someone else had disturbed her possessions. It was ridiculous, really. She'd made sure to lock her chamber door with her own locks, and she was the only person with the key.

She had been especially diligent about locking her door since the people here had already proven to be so appallingly dishonest.

A first search failed to turn up her journal. She determined to be careful on her second effort, but still her journal wasn't there.

Her heart nearly thumped out of her chest when she realized her suspicions had been correct. Someone had been in her chamber. Someone had gone through her portmanteau.

Someone had stolen her travel journal.

She leapt up, fearing that person might still be in her chamber. The room was too small to hide anyone—unless they were under the bed. Trembling uncontrollably, she approached her bed and bent to peek beneath it.

She wished she hadn't. No one was there, but she pitied the poor person who would try to lie in that filth. Either the inn had no one to clean, or the cleaner was supremely inefficient.

Assured she was alone, she began to search through her things to see what else was missing. She'd brought no jewels since being warned against traveling with them. She didn't even wear any because that would alert thieves of her wealth.

She went first to the leather pouch where she stored her passport and some of the local currency. To her relief, it was still there. What kind of thief wasn't interested in money?

She searched through the portmanteau as well as her valise and was relatively certain nothing else had been stolen.

Even though she knew without a doubt the intruder was gone, she couldn't stop shaking. Why would someone steal her journal? She'd written no more than twenty pages in it.

Intrinsically, she knew its disappearance had to be tied to the disappearance of Miss Willets.

That was it! The person responsible for abducting Miss Willets feared Mary had written about her companion, and he was out to destroy any evidence that the woman had ever commenced on this journey. Even though Mary had not written very much, the culprit would not have wanted to risk discovery by taking the time to read what she had written.

She stood there in her chamber, her eyes watering, her whole body shaking. Who had done this? It couldn't have been the Frenchmen because she was absolutely certain they had been in the eating room while the theft was being committed.

Exonerating them made her feel even lower. They had been the most obvious suspects in Miss Willets' disappearance because they had been the only other travelers in the group since the beginning. And they had lied.

Had this happened to her in London, she would have had Devere. She would have had access to magistrates. But here, no one believed her. Everyone was against her. Except for Lord Stephen Stanhope.

She must go to him. But she had no idea which was his of the inn's fourteen chambers—yes, she had counted them. Then there was the garret where the guests' servants slept.

She must find Lord Stephen.

ACTING AS CASUAL as he could, Stephen stopped to chat with Becker when he returned to the ground floor. There was little to recommend most of the innkeepers Stephen had encountered on this journey, but Becker was far and away the best. Not only were his accommodations superior to the others, but he was much friendlier.

French seemed to be the universal language in use throughout these mountains. "Since you've obviously had a great deal of experience with these snowstorms, I'm interested to hear when you think things might clear. I have important business in Vienna," Stephen said.

"Well, if it were late January or February, I'd say to be prepared to stay at Le Chateau for several weeks. Of course, in late January or early February, only a fool would attempt such a journey. It's rare if we even have a single guest then. But these December storms, I must say, are not as severe, nor is their duration as long. My guess is that we'll be able to dig out of here in a day or two—if the snow would just stop falling."

"That's a big *if* judging by the intensity of today's snowfall."

"Be assured, my friend, it will stop. One must be patient. At least you have a lovely woman with whom to pass the time. You must take advantage of this gift few men are ever afforded."

Stephen smiled. "She is lovely."

"What serendipity that you and she should have met here in what many of my guests refer to as *the middle of nowhere*. You two were previously acquainted, no?"

Stephen hesitated before answering. He wanted to tell the partial truth that their families were acquainted, but hadn't Lady Mary wished him to claim a previous friendship? He wouldn't lie. "Yes. Our families have long been acquainted."

"Ah, my lord, you are a most fortunate man."

Becker was saying this even though he insisted Lady Mary was mentally confused.

Perhaps Stephen should act upon the man's suggestion. Perhaps Stephen should take this opportunity to cultivate the lady's more amorous instincts. He could not deny he would enjoy having Lady Mary warming his bed.

But, of course, she was a lady, the sister of a worthy man. He could never seduce such a woman.

As much as he would like to.

The striking of feet upon the wooden stairs came closer, and Stephen looked up to see Lady Mary. Her face had gone white, and she appeared upset. Gravely so.

He rushed to her, taking her elbow and steering her to the inglenook, which he knew to be unoccupied. She was trembling, and he feared she was about to burst into tears. "What's the matter?" he whispered.

He insisted she sit nearest the fire, and he sat beside her. She needed a good warming.

"Someone's been in my room."

He believed her. Not even the exuberant Lady Mary could feign such distress. "Did you not lock it?"

"Of course I locked it. I brought my own locks from England, and I'm the only one with the key."

She was too upset for him to broach an argument. Later, he would examine her locks and disprove her claim that she had secured her chamber.

"You shouldn't travel with jewels. You can't trust anyone at these inns."

She glared at him. "I did not travel with my jewels. I am not an idiot."

"What was stolen?"

"The only thing missing was my travel journal."

He began to laugh.

Which made her burst into tears. These weren't just a few teardrops sliding down her remarkable face. These were full-fledged sobs, wracking her entire body.

He felt wretched. He couldn't bear to see a woman cry. Acting purely on instinct, his arm settled gently on her heaving shoulders. She collapsed against him, burying her face into his chest. His other arm came around her, and he began to trace soothing circles on her shaking back.

As much as he wanted to, he was incapable of finding the words that would assure her. He wanted to vow that nothing could ever happen to her as long as he was here, but he could not make a pledge he might not be able to fulfill—not that he wouldn't make every effort to protect her.

Oddly, even knowing her dramatic qualities and still doubtful of the existence of Miss Willets, he believed Lady Mary Beresford now. The most gifted actress could not convey the emotions that now consumed her.

And the most profound of those emotions was fear.

He felt it as palpably as the fire blazing not six feet from them.

Though this lady was his chief concern, he could not deny how good it felt to hold her in his arms. Her delicacy and neediness tugged at his elemental protectiveness. *I will do everything in my power to take care of her.*

"I'm so sorry this has happened to you," he murmured.

She whimpered. "I've never been so frightened." Sniff. Sniff. "Except when the avalanche narrowly missed us."

"On this trip?"

She nodded and straightened herself. "I'm surprised you didn't hear Miss Willets' and me scream even though you were a day's travel behind. It was dreadful."

He was glad she was getting her mind off her recent distress. Even though he'd enjoyed holding her in his arms.

He produced a handkerchief and handed it to her.

She offered a feeble smile. "I don't know what I would have done on this journey without you."

"I've done nothing."

"But in you, I have a friend. A confidant." She dabbed her tears with the handkerchief, then turned away to daintily blow her nose. When she turned back, she offered him a smile. Even with eyes and nose red, she was the loveliest woman he'd ever seen.

"I'm sorry I laughed when you told me your journal was stolen." His flippancy was responsible for her crying fit. "I just found it improbable that a thief would steal something so . . . worthless."

"I agree," she said with great solemnity. "The only thing that explains it is that the person responsible for Miss Willets' disappearance feared I'd written about her. He's intent on wiping out anything that would point to the lady's existence."

It all sounded perfectly logical. *If there had been a Miss Willets.* "Are you certain nothing else was stolen?"

She shook her pretty little head. Her eyes began to water again. "He didn't even touch my money."

A most peculiar thief, to be sure.

As much as he did not want to believe the preposterous story about the theft from her chamber, he believed her now. "I would like to inspect your locks."

She nodded solemnly.

Together, they climbed to the third level. Both the second and third levels were laid out identically in a U shape around the stairwell. Lady Mary's chamber was the last one to the right of the landing.

"Who's in the chamber next to you?" he asked.

"No one, as far as I can tell, even though Mr. Lying Becker claims full occupancy."

He examined the lock she had clamped to the door, then he asked for her key. The locks were much the same as the ones he used. Everything seemed to be in working order. He had never had any complaints about the efficacy of his locks. He couldn't help but to wonder if she'd forgotten to lock it when she left her chamber.

He looked down into her melancholy face. "You're absolutely certain you locked the chamber when you went to breakfast?"

"I know it doesn't seem plausible to you, but the reason I'm so sure is that I distinctly remember that I had difficulty opening the lock when I returned to the room."

He wondered if there was another way to gain entrance to her room. "May I come into your chamber? We can leave the door open."

She stepped aside. "Of course."

Halfway into the room, he stopped and surveyed his surroundings. The layout of the room was identical to his. Even the furnishings of four-poster bed, night stand, settle, clothes press, and small writing table were the same. Items of clothing were scattered about the room. He presumed she had done that. He noted that her portmanteau was standing open, presumably as she'd left it when she fled downstairs in a state of near hysteria.

He strode to the window and opened it. A rush of cold air swooshed into the chamber. He leaned out. Since she was on a corner, there was just one window near hers, but there was no way someone from the next chamber could have come in this window even though it didn't lock. It was a three-story drop to the snow below, and there was nothing on which to stand between the two rooms.

He closed the window, turned to her, and shrugged. "I believe you, but I don't know how anyone could have gotten in here."

"I agree. It's distressingly baffling."

Their eyes met and, for that single moment, he felt a deep connection to her. Even if he'd never spoken to Devere, he would have wanted to help her. "Would it comfort you if I could persuade Becker to give me the room next to yours?"

Once more, her eyes filled with tears. "Oh, yes, please!"

CHAPTER SIX

W HY IN THE devil would a thief only be interested in Lady Mary's journal? And how in the devil had someone been able to break into her chamber? Stephen descended the stairs at a much slower pace than normal as he pondered these perplexing questions.

The inn did not have an actual reception area, but Becker could often be found in what passed for a reception. Now that Stephen was seeking him, though, Becker was not there. Stephen swept past the inglenook. No one was there, either. In the eating room he noted that the Belgians had joined the French brothers to play whist. Stephen nodded, then left the chamber.

By the time he reached what he'd come to think of as Becker's area, the innkeeper was just entering through a door which Stephen presumed to be his private chambers. "Bonjour," Becker said, smiling.

"Ah, just the man I want to see." Stephen had decided he would play into Becker's own suggestion about a romantic dalliance with Lady Mary. He came closer to Becker and dropped his voice. "It would mean a great deal to me if I could take possession of the chamber next to the English lady."

Becker had claimed that all chambers were occupied; Lady Mary swore that no one had been in her neighboring chamber. One of them was lying, and he was almost certain that this time it was Becker.

Stephen produced a gold coin and set it on the table that separated the two men. "I'm willing to pay for anyone's inconvenience."

Becker's eyes flashed, his mouth lifted into a smile. "I think that can be managed, my lord." He pocketed the coin. "I'll have the porter move your things into the chamber this afternoon, if that will be agreeable to you."

"Most agreeable—though I won't need a porter. My man can move my things."

❯❯❯❯❮❮❮❮

MOMENTS LATER, MARY met him in the inglenook. "Well?" she asked even before she sat.

"It appears, my lady, we are going to be neighbors."

She took the place he'd saved for her closest to the fire. "I daresay you were obliged to cross his palm with silver."

"Gold, not silver."

"He's a terrible man." She looked up into Stephen's dark eyes. "I shall be enormously indebted to you."

"Becker believes we're lovers."

Her heartbeat quickened. There was something in Lord Stephen's tone she'd not heard before—a huskiness that conveyed intimacy. And not the kind of intimacy she shared with Sophia.

Then it occurred to her that perhaps his kindness to her stemmed from his desire to seduce her. He was a man, after all.

No matter how appealing he was, no matter how grateful she was to him, she would not ruin herself to show him her gratitude. "It's likely a good thing that dreadful man believes that. Good for me, since he does seem to favor you."

"What makes you think he favors me?" he asked.

She shrugged. "I can just tell. Have you not noticed that it's always the tall men over whom everyone always fawns? You are blessed to be tall. It's not just women who favor you, but other men also look up to you—and I mean that figuratively as well as literally."

"You cannot substantiate one bit of that."

"Why should I? It's true."

"Has anyone ever told you you're maddening?"

"My brother. Daily."

"If you were my sister I'd lock you in your bedchamber."

She giggled. "Devere does threaten that all the time."

"At least you had the good sense to bring locks. But for the life of me, I cannot understand how someone got into your chamber. You said you had difficulty unlocking when you returned from breakfast? Was that the first time you'd had difficulty?"

"Yes."

"It does seem as if someone must have tampered with your lock." He stopped as the girl with the thick blonde braids came to toss another log on the inglenook's fire. There looked to be a month's worth of logs stacked floor to ceiling beside the hearth.

After the girl left, he continued. "What gall one would have to possess to risk getting caught finagling your lock. Who else is on your floor?"

"I'm not really certain. I have seen the Italian couple, and I believe the Belgians who traveled with you are there, though the only ones I've actually seen enter or leave a chamber on my floor are the Italians."

"Where do our chair men sleep?"

"Not in this building. They're scattered in the cottages near the stables."

He frowned. "So, given the depth of the snow surrounding us, we'll not be able to question them further at this time."

"I am so out of charity with them. I couldn't believe they would lie about poor Miss Willets—and defy me. I assure you, I've been most kindly toward them throughout this journey." She pouted. "And you're sickeningly right about us not being able to further question them. I will own, I had thought I might have been able to coax the truth out of them."

He looked askance at her, his eyes flashing with mirth. "You are one cocky lady."

"I cannot deny it. It comes from being the middle sister. I had to distinguish myself in some way. I chose to be supremely confident. But," she looked up at him, turning deadly serious. "I am not so confident that I would refuse any assistance you give me."

"I do want to help you. You must agree, though, that it's difficult to credit anyone would wish to harm a small, elderly, congenial lady."

He looked at her as if he believed her delusional. She bristled. "Are you, too, intimating that I'm queer in the attic?"

"I don't believe that at all. Quite the opposite. You are clever."

"If I were clever, I ought to be able to find Miss Willets. The only explanation that suits is my fantastic story that she's some princess in hiding."

"You may be on the right trail. It could be that something from her past has threatened her existence, but I doubt she was royalty in disguise."

She wondered if he was just saying that to please her. Had he come to believe her about Miss Willets? "Perhaps she knew her last employer committed a crime, and he wishes to kill her to keep her silent."

He chuckled. "You are possessed of a lively imagination."

"Don't. Go. There." She glared at him. Was he just like the rest of the disbelievers? Yet those disgusting creatures were more than disbelievers. They were outright liars. Even her own chair men.

"No matter how much we try to hypothesize the lady's disappearance, it doesn't help us to find her, does it?" he asked.

"No. And the pity of it is we can't even get to the stables or to those ominous cottages to look for her."

"She could be in the inn."

Did he believe her, or was he merely humoring her? "My fear is that she's been killed," she said, her voice shaking.

"If only there was proof of her existence. Then it would be easier to confront those who you say have lied."

His words crushed her. *You say*. He did not believe her, after all. He was merely being gallant. Which, in some odd way, comforted her. She would have preferred that he believed her, but two days ago he didn't even know of her existence. It was unrealistic to expect total loyalty from a stranger. As it was, she should erect a shrine to this man for his many kindnesses in the face of his skepticism.

"My journal would not necessarily have proven that we were traveling companions."

He nodded. "Because you could still have written of her after she went missing."

"Yes. But I believe if her cards could be found, they could prove she was with us. To my knowledge those dastardly Frenchies never returned them."

"And what did the cards look like?"

"They featured pretty pastel-colored birds against a pale blue sky."

"Still, if they lied once, they could just lie and say they've had the cards all along."

He was right, disgustingly so.

He eyed her. "Did she, perchance, own something valuable? Something worth killing for?"

"I would kill for her furry boots!" She instantly regretted her words. The dear governess had pledged to leave them to Mary in her will. Mary sighed. She would far rather have the pink-cheeked lady here than her coveted boots.

His face went deadly serious as he stared at her.

She threw up her hands. "I jest."

Shaking his head, he smiled. "I shall never understand the workings of the female mind."

"Seriously, how could a governess own anything of great value?" she asked.

"There is that."

She scooted a wee bit closer, lowered her voice, and said, "Another suspicious thing about the Italians . . . they speak nothing but Italian."

"It is unusual for the wealthier Italians not to speak French, but perhaps they've not always been wealthy? And Becker is sure to be able to speak in their tongue."

"Do you?"

"Speak Italian?"

She nodded.

"Of course. That's why I was chosen for the Foreign Office."

"What languages do you speak?"

"The usual. French, German, Italian, Spanish. And then there's Latin and ancient Greek."

He was even more educated than Devere, who spoke only French and German—and, of course, read Latin and Greek. She supposed as a younger son of a duke, Lord Stephen had been destined for the Foreign Office, where a command of languages would be essential.

"Then you'll be able to communicate with the Italians?" she asked hopefully.

"I suppose I could, but surely you don't think they know anything about your Miss Willets. Did you not say they weren't of your party?"

"That's true, but the Frenchmen who were in my party have now been eliminated. They couldn't have been responsible for stealing my journal because they were all in the eating room when it was stolen. And . . . the Italians are on the same floor as me."

He did not respond for a moment. "Should you like me to search their rooms the next time they go to the eating room?"

"Surely they would not be so trusting as to not lock it when they leave."

"I would, of course, have to see what kind of lock they use. If they merely rely on what exists on the doors, I believe I can manage to open it."

Her brows lifted. "My, my, this duke's son is possessed of nefarious talents."

"I'll see what I can learn. Expect me to be late for dinner."

Words were inadequate to express her appreciation.

>>>><<<<

HUMPHREY HAD BROUGHT Stephen's possessions to the chamber next to Lady Mary's. To his knowledge, no one had been displaced—which begged the question *Why would Becker be lying about having a guest in each chamber?*

There appeared to be fourteen guest rooms. The Italians shared one, and the other six guests each claimed a chamber. That left seven rooms with no guests. And, of course, the guests' servants were quartered up in the garret. Lady Mary had said the chair men and porters slept in the cottages. Who, then, occupied the other chambers?

Stephen stood patiently as Humphrey tied his cravat. "If I may say so, my lord, it pleases me that you will look the proper gentleman tonight."

Stephen eyed the valet who'd been with him every day for more than a decade. He was some half a dozen years older than Stephen, but Stephen had not noticed before that the slender fellow's hair was threaded with silver. When in the devil had that happened?

After Humphrey finished with him and left, Stephen strode to the window of his new chamber and peered out. Dusk was falling. Something else had occurred since he'd last looked at the village-like setting that surrounded Le Chateau. The porters had begun to try to dig a path from the largest of the cottages to the inn. They would not be able to finish before it became completely dark. He supposed the men who slept there were running out of food.

Becker had told him Le Chateau had a huge larder and enough stores put away to last through the winter.

Soon, the guests would be making their way downstairs to the eating room. A door opened on the opposite side of the stairwell from his chamber, and he heard the Italians disparaging that there would no doubt be more cheeses for the dinner offerings.

Not long afterward, Lady Mary left her chamber. He knew how difficult it was for her to sit alone in the eating room filled with people she perceived as her enemies. For her sake, he was glad Devere had asked him to take care of his sister. And if it hadn't been for the possibly fictional Miss Willets, Stephen never would have caught up with her.

Another door opened, this one next to him. He moved to listen. He thought it was Blanchard. After taking a few steps, the man knocked on another door. Stephen recognized the voices of Blanchard and Dubois. The two then descended the stairs together.

Since Lady Mary was not sure if there was anyone else on her floor, he had to wait and see if anyone else was leaving. He waited five more minutes, and then he tiptoed from his chamber, locking the door behind him.

He went to the door Lady Mary had pointed to as belonging to the Italians, thankful the guide books available in Italy must not recommend the bringing of one's own locks. The ones Le Chateau provided could easily be jimmied.

In less than sixty seconds, he was in, quietly opening and closing the door. He needed to be quick, but he had no idea what he was looking for. Lady Mary's journal? Playing cards with pastel birds? A little old lady stuffed into the clothing press?

The layout of the room and furnishings were identical to his and Lady Mary's, except this bed was larger. He looked under the bed, and his estimation of Becker's innkeeping sank.

Two portmanteaus were open, one with male clothing and the other with feminine finery, including fur boots. He chuckled to himself that Lady Mary said she would kill for furry boots.

Even the idea of searching through a lady's private clothing made him feel like a lecher, but he would do it for Lady Mary. He executed the search as quickly and neatly as possible, but he found nothing that piqued his interest.

Then he did the same with the male's portmanteau, which was stuffed with fine clothing and a book. He examined it. Its title was *Guide to European Travel*, and it was written in French. Hmmm. Hadn't they pretended not to speak anything but Italian? Why would they lie about something like that?

He went next to the linen press, which held the couple's outer garments, all heavy woolens. On its top was a mirror, shaving equipment, and a lady's hairbrush.

Before leaving the chamber, for curiosity's sake he moved to the bedside table to examine the book there. He opened it and began flipping through the pages. Good Lord! He'd not seen such pornographic drawings since Blinky Whitehead had passed a dog-eared volume among their randy school chums at Eton.

He quickly closed it.

All in all, he'd risked much for nil. Had he been caught, he would have been branded a thief.

He couldn't get out of there fast enough.

As soon as he shut the door, he heard footsteps on the stairs.

CHAPTER SEVEN

S TEPHEN HAD NOT yet relocked the Italians' door, but he couldn't risk being found there, either, and he was already late to dinner. He had no choice but to hurry down the stairs.

One of the Frenchmen from Lady Mary's party turned into the landing of the second level, smiling up at him. "I forgot to bring my knife," he explained to Stephen. "Tonight's meat is very tough."

"I try to never go off without mine." Stephen wondered if Lady Mary also carried a knife in that reticule of hers. Because she had brought her own locks, he believed she'd read the same guide books he had—besides that rare copy of William Beckford's he'd found so interesting.

When he entered the eating room, she looked up and smiled. His food awaited him across the table from her. He still trembled from the scare of almost being found exiting the Italians' room.

"I fear your food's cold," she said as he settled into his chair.

Since the Frenchmen's table was just across the hearth from theirs, he spoke in a loud enough voice for them to hear, though, as was his custom with her, he spoke in English. "Did you see that the porters are digging a path from their cottage to Le Chateau? I got delayed watching them."

"Really?" she said with enthusiasm.

He nodded. "They'll probably finish in the morning." He

withdrew his knife and began to cut the boiled gray meat. He didn't want to know what animal it had been.

"Do you have something interesting to report?" she asked in a whisper.

"Very little." He washed down the tasteless meat with a swallow of wine. He didn't want to know the origins of the wine, either. It was wretched. "One thing of interest."

Her fine brows elevated. She was exquisite. How she managed to look so elegant in such a rustic setting without the assistance of a lady's maid was a testament to her natural beauty.

Though he knew little about women's fashions, he realized she must have brought a sizable wardrobe of fashionable gowns. She'd worn a different dress each time he saw her.

She could have graced London's—or Vienna's—finest ballrooms in the delicate creation she wore tonight. He noted appreciatively how the ivory dress displayed her creamy white shoulders and the rise of her breasts. A woman this stunning had no need for the brilliance of jewels.

"Their guide book is written in French," he continued in a whisper.

Her face crumbled. "You see, everyone is against me! More liars. You are the only person in this unimaginably detestable place who tells the truth!"

He felt as guilty as the others who had deceived her. He prayed she would never learn Devere had sent him after her.

She sounded so completely inflamed it was difficult not to believe her accusations. He shrugged. "I'm sorry."

He noted that she had, indeed, brought her own knife, one with a mother-of-pearl handle. It suited her. He fleetingly thought it could also double as a weapon, if the need should ever arise.

He set down his knife and fork. "I encountered a problem."

"Pray, do not tell me you were discovered."

"Almost. As I was attempting to relock their chamber door, I heard footsteps coming up the stairs."

With a dramatic flair, her eyes shuttered. "I cringed when I saw one of those Frenchies leave the next table," she whispered. "I tried to think of some way to distract him, but he was gone from the room before I could. Was he on our floor?"

"Thankfully, no. But I didn't know that when I heard footsteps climbing the stairs." He sighed. "I had to leave before I was able to relock their door."

She winced. "Oh, no. You're sure to be the first person they suspect when they discover their room unlocked, given that you came here so late."

"I am aware of that. My only hope is that they'll think they forgot to lock it."

"That's an awfully unlikely-to-be-fulfilled hope."

"Thank you for your reassurance."

A tender expression on her face, she set her hand on his. "I'm most dreadfully sorry for involving you in my own distresses. You're like a knight of yore, coming to a maiden's rescue."

He was not unaffected either by her touch or her praise. No woman had ever likened him to a knight of yore. He felt as if he'd grown a foot taller.

"Will there be a sign in their chamber, do you think, to alert them that their room's been searched?" She had kept her voice a whisper.

"I don't think so. I tried to be careful. Respectful." He wouldn't tell her about the erotic book. It could have no possible bearing on her investigation.

She removed her hand from his and took a sip of wine, scrunching her nose as she did. "I just cannot comprehend why every single person here is lying."

"Nor can I." This was perhaps the first time he could not question her allegations. As far as the Italians were concerned, he, too, had witnessed their refusal to speak any language other than Italian. Why would they have reason to lie?

Though he would never admit it to Lady Mary, he still had doubts about the veracity of her belief that Becker, the chair men, and the Frenchmen all were lying about Miss Willets. There was no plausible explanation for such a conspiracy against Lady Mary.

And there was also her brother's allegation about her propensity to not always be honest.

Yet . . . he could think of no reason why she would have invented the existence of a jolly little governess who'd vanished, especially since she was so distressed about it.

He wished he knew more about the Italians. Had they actually chosen to come to Le Chateau for a winter holiday? Becker would know.

Stephen decided he needed to cultivate a friendship of sorts with the innkeeper. He smiled to himself at the memory of Lady Mary's belief that Becker favored him, that tall men merited more admiration than men of lesser stature.

He wondered if she was one of those who admired men of above-average height.

>>><<<

AFTER DINNER MARY and Stephen once again claimed the inglenook. "Whenever I marry," she said, "I shall have an inglenook built in my home. I've become very fond of them. Is there anything more cozy?"

"I don't suppose there is. Speaking of marriage, are you like Lady Sophia?"

"In what way?"

"It's common knowledge your beautiful sister turned down dozens of proposals of marriage. How many have you turned down, my lady?"

Her lashes lowered coyly. The truth was she had turned down more than a dozen proposals, including one from a duke, but she felt that admitting to such would make her sound boastful, and she abhorred those who bragged.

Worse yet, she feared that her refusal to marry might make her seem as if she thought herself above the men who had offered.

She was unaccountably flattered that he had asked such a question. She wanted to convey modesty, so she did not look at him. She merely shrugged. "A lady does not discuss such personal matters."

"I think I know the answer."

Now she looked up and boldly eyed him. "What about you, my lord? Have you ever offered for a young lady?"

He shook his head. "I am not much in Society."

"Are you that married to your duties?"

"I suppose I am. It pleases me to serve my country. I'll be happy when the Congress has concluded, and we'll once again be able to have embassies throughout the European capitals. I've always been lured by the promise of residing in other countries."

He perfectly described her own aspirations. "Is there one you'd especially like?"

He smiled. "When I was a lad, Sir William Hamilton's long posting in Naples fascinated me. Everything about Naples, from the active volcano to the antiquities to the sea splashing at its shores, has always lured me. And, of course, the near perpetual sunshine after dreary old England has a strong pull."

She nodded empathetically. She would adore Naples. "I remember how upset my father was when Napoleon claimed Naples. I share the strong pull to see that ancient kingdom."

"I doubt it will be a kingdom again. Liberty reigns."

"We have liberty, and we have a king."

"A king without power."

"Our poor king is without a mind, too."

His lips folded into a grim line. "But we do have a spendthrift regent."

"You don't approve of our regent?"

"I support the monarchy."

She smiled. "I can see you were destined for a career in diplomacy."

"And just what is it Lady Sophia's husband does in Vienna? Is he attached to the Congress?"

"No. I'm not quite certain what it is Will does. His family has one of the largest banks in Vienna—and England—and he has something to do with that, though he is rather on the move a lot. Which Sophia adores."

"Are you like Sophia in that respect, too?"

She did not know if being like Sophia would be admirable in his eyes or not. She did know she wanted more than anything for Lord Stephen Stanhope to admire her. "I have always wanted to travel throughout Europe. Is that not obvious? One would have to be most determined to strike off on her own across the Continent without even her lady's maid."

"A woman after my own heart."

Their eyes locked. Her heartbeat accelerated. It had been such a simple statement but, to her, it was . . . romantic. Since the moment she had met him, she had not allowed herself to admit she was attracted to him.

But, God in His Heavenly Kingdom, she was!

She had tried to dissuade herself. She had tried to think of flaws in his character or flaws in his appearance, but there were none—other than the possible fact he did not entirely believe her about Miss Willets. But that he championed her even not fully believing her made him all the more heroic. She'd spoken the truth when she likened him to a gallant medieval knight.

For once in her life, Mary was unable to speak.

Did he regret his words? He soon looked away and stared at the hearth. "How long do you suppose one has to chop trees to get a stack of firewood that tall?"

He did regret his praise—praise she had so needily and greedily welcomed. "It is not a matter upon which I'd waste my thoughts."

"You wound me, accusing me of wasted thinking."

"Forgive me if it sounded as if I thought you capable of idle thoughts. Certainly one who speaks as many languages as you possesses rigorous mental discipline."

Now that she had complimented him, she turned her attention to the flames, her thoughts melancholy. Why were all these
people saying she had imagined Miss Willets? What could possess
them to lie? And what frightening fate had befallen poor Miss
Willets?

She felt him staring at her and looked up into his black eyes.

"Why so forlorn?" he asked.

"You know."

"Would you like me to question your French traveling companions?"

"They'll just tell you I was sick and delusional, that I made up
an imaginary companion."

"I've seen nothing about you to substantiate such a claim."

She could have thrown her arms around him. "Then, yes, I
would like you to speak with them. Surely you'll be able to
determine if they're lying."

"I'll come down to breakfast earlier than you tomorrow, and
I'll confront them then."

"Do you think you might permit yourself to . . . stretch the
truth a bit?"

His dark brows lowered as he eyed her sternly. "By saying
what?"

"That you've known me for a long time, and I've never displayed any symptoms of irrationality."

"I won't lie for you, Mary."

He'd called her by her Christian name. *No Lady Mary*. No
man, other than her brother, had ever addressed her in such a
way in her one-and-twenty years.

That single omission lowered a barrier between them. Their
connection deepened—even though he refused to lie for her.

"One should not lie to reveal the truth," he said. "We mustn't
sink to their depths."

At least he was finally talking as if he just might believe her.

Now that he'd shown her his reverence for the truth, she
admired him even more. Lord Stephen Stanhope was a man who

valued morality.

"You're right, and you make me ashamed. I admit, in the past, I have stretched the truth a wee bit to achieve my goals, but I swear on my dear father's grave, I'm not lying about Miss Willets' disappearance, and I don't think I shall ever lie again."

He took her hand and pressed it reassuringly. "I'll talk to the Frenchmen tomorrow morning."

His very touch had the power to quicken her pulse and send a smoldering heat through her entire body.

CHAPTER EIGHT

T HAT NIGHT AS she lay in her bed, she feared the wind's ferocity would level the timbered inn. The building quivered, and the odd tree limb would slam into it, preventing her from sleep.

She wanted to look from her window and see how hard the snow was pounding down, but she was too comfortable beneath the heavy eiderdown she'd pulled up to her chin.

It wasn't just the snowstorm that had kept her awake. She'd been unable to purge Stephen from her thoughts. He had tenderly pressed her hand. He had called her Mary. He was beginning to truly believe her.

Was she reading too much into his actions? Was he merely being gallant? Or was he coming to care for her in the same way she was coming to care for him?

In the four years since she had come out, she had turned down thirteen offers of marriage. All of the men had been worthy, but she had vowed to follow Sophia's example and not settle for a prospective husband merely to be married to a worthy man. She wanted a man who evoked a knight of yore.

Sophia had avoided marriage all those years because she was waiting for the one man in the universe who'd been created just for her. She believed that when she met that being she would instantly feel it. And she had known it the night she'd met Will

Birmingham.

Mary understood now. Now that she'd met Lord Stephen Stanhope. She felt as if she'd waited her whole life for this man. Now—under monumentally oppressive circumstances—she had found that one man who had been destined for her.

As worried as she was about Miss Willets, and as upset as she was that all the inhabitants of Le Chateau were against her, Mary came to realize that had Miss Willets not disappeared, she would never have met Stephen. Miss Willets' tragic disappearance had been Mary's fate.

Could he possibly feel it, too?

THE FIERCE SNOWSTORM had awakened him early. All those cold mornings at Eton had inured him to biting chills. He left his bed, went to the window, and shook his head ruefully. The path the porters had dug the previous day had all but disappeared.

Damn but it was cold! He tossed a pair of logs on the embers and fiddled with kindling until the flames caught. He would not disturb Humphrey on so cold a morning. He quickly dressed himself in his warmest clothing and tall, fur-lined boots.

What would lovely Mary wear today? Surely not one of those thin gowns that displayed her ivory shoulders and the promise of her womanly breasts. If she possessed the sense he had come to credit her with, she would wear woolens. Layers of them.

Even though it was still quite dark, he was determined to be the first in the eating room. He intended to strike up a conversation with the Frenchmen who'd traveled with Mary, and during the conversation he would introduce the topic of Miss Willets.

On the way to the eating room he thought about his refusal last night to lie for her. What a bloody hypocrite he was! His entire presence here was a lie. He prayed his efforts to help her would in some way compensate for his deception though God

LADY MARY'S DANGEROUS ENCOUNTER

knows those efforts fell damned short of assuaging his conscience.

A fire already blazed in the hearth when he entered the chamber. The girl with the blonde braids must be an early riser. He sat at their regular table, the scrape of his chair on the wood floors making enough noise to alert the girl to his presence.

A moment later, she entered the room, carrying a pot of hot water and a cup for his tea. Sounds of activity continued from the adjacent kitchen. The cook.

He wondered if the girl in braids was Becker's daughter. And the unseen cook? Would that, perchance, be Becker's wife? Surely the man must be wed. Winters here would be exceedingly long and lonely without a partner.

Through the window that faced the front of the inn, he was able to observe the rise of bleak daylight amidst the incessant falling of snow. It was then that one of the Frenchmen who'd traveled with Mary came into the room and sat at the next table.

"*Bonjour*," Stephen said.

The man, who was perhaps five to ten years older than Stephen's thirty years, looked up and smiled. "*Bonjour.*"

Stephen grabbed his cup and moved to the other table. "Do you mind if I join you?" he asked in French.

"Please do."

Though most Frenchmen Stephen had known tended to be slender, this man was short and muscular with upper arms like cannonballs. It occurred to Stephen that even though he was half a foot taller than this man, the Frenchman might be capable of besting him in a fight.

Soon the girl brought the Frenchman coffee, then returned a moment later with two plates of breads and cheeses with the added luxury of a hard-cooked egg for each.

While they ate, Stephen struck up a conversation. "By the way, I am Lord Stephen Stanhope."

"Ah, an aristocrat!" the man said with smile. "I am merely plain Pierre Fontaine, traveling with my brother. We travel together."

"What part of France do you call home?"

The man hesitated a moment. "Paris."

"I look forward to seeing your fine city now that the war is over."

The Frenchman's expression was inscrutable. "It is very fine, the most beautiful city in all of Europe, but I may not be impartial."

"So what is your destination?" Stephen asked.

"Do we all not go to Vienna?"

The other brother joined them, and Pierre handled the introductions. Unlike his brother, Charles was slender, closer to Stephen's height, and at least five years older than Stephen. Gray sprinkled through his warm brown hair the same shade as his brother's.

Within a moment, the girl brought him coffee and food.

"What is it you are going to Vienna for?" Stephen asked.

"The Congress, of course," Pierre answered.

"You serve Tallyrand?"

Pierre hesitated, and before he could answer, the brother Stephen suspected was the elder said they did.

Since Stephen had spent most nights of this long journey educating himself on all the members of the Congress and their goals and accomplishments thus far, he was confident in his knowledge of it.

He continued to ask questions about the Frenchmen and their roles in the Congress, but he was not satisfied with their answers.

Neither of them knew anything about the conference. Moreover, they did not even speak court French, as would any Frenchman associated in any way with international diplomacy.

These men were lying.

If they lied about their mission, they could easily have lied about Miss Willets.

Good Lord! Was Stephen in agreement with Lady Mary? Was he coming to believe her wild accusations? In spite of the preposterousness of her claims, she had far more credibility than these shady men.

"Say," Stephen said, swigging his tea and then leaning forward and lowering his voice as if he were about to make a monumental declaration, "tell me about the old woman who's disappeared."

To a man, their eyes rounded. "We know of no such woman," Charles snapped.

Pierre Fontaine, who in spite of the disparity in their builds looked remarkably like his brother, looked at Stephen with contempt. "Your English companion was very ill. Her sickness made her hallucinate."

Stephen had to show great restraint not to throw a fist into the Frenchman's smug mouth. The man was a liar. However sick Mary had been upon her arrival, she was perfectly recovered now. And she was lucid. A hell of a lot more so than these frauds.

Years of training in diplomacy enabled him to hide his true feelings, smile at them, and shrug. "You know what women are."

Now they smiled.

"Perhaps sometime you will permit me to join you in a game of whist," Stephen said, rising from his chair as he noted Mary elegantly gliding into the chamber.

"We should welcome it." Charles said.

Stephen greeted Mary, pleased to see that she had displayed good judgment and donned a royal blue woolen dress with a high, lace-trimmed neckline, and she'd covered it with a red Kashmir shawl. Her hair was swept back, and somehow she had contrived to look as fresh as a spring primrose. "You look lovely this morning," he greeted. "Did you sleep well?"

She lowered herself into the chair he held out for her, rolling her eyes. "The wretched storm awakened me. What about you?'

"I always sleep well, but I did awaken earlier than normal. Did you see that the path from the cottage has been eradicated?"

She nodded grimly. "I wonder if we'll ever be able to leave Le Chateau."

The girl with braids brought her a pot of boiling water and a plate of food, and Mary busied herself making her tea while casually dropping her voice and asking in a whisper, "How has your morning gone?"

In an equally low voice, he said, "We'll discuss it after breakfast."

MARY HAD BEEN in a hurry to finish breakfast and be able to speak candidly with Stephen. How she hated being surrounded by all these imminently detestable people.

Because she and Stephen were the first to leave the eating chamber, they were able to claim the inglenook, where a freshly built fire warmed the entire cubicle. She took her customary seat next to the hearth and then whipped around to face him. "Well?"

"The Frenchmen are liars."

She sat frozen for a moment, allowing the impact of his words to sink in. Then she favored him with a wide smile. "It's gratifying to know I'm being vindicated. How were you able to determine they lied about Miss Willets?"

"Though my acquaintance with you is not of long duration, I will never believe that you hallucinate."

"So that's what those falsehood-telling, foul-tongued French frauds are saying about me?"

A slow grin spread across Stephen's manly face, and his dark eyes flashed with humor as he regarded her. "I must remember not to invoke your disfavor, my lady." He chuckled. "Indeed, that is what your French companions say. And that is not their only falsehood."

She moved closer, close enough for her to breathe in his masculine sandalwood scent. Everything about this man bespoke power from his commanding height to the breadth of his shoulders and the rock-hard heft of his thighs straining against his chocolate woolen breeches—and most of all, the solidity of his character. What a credit he was to their country's Foreign Office. "Pray, do tell me all."

"Have you not noticed the men don't speak court French?"

"I daresay I've not spoken to the vile men, but what does it matter if they are commoners?"

"They claim to be going to the Congress in Vienna."

"That does put a different spin on things, does it not? Why do you suppose they would fabricate such a tale?"

He shrugged. "I would have to be clairvoyant to answer your question."

"I wish one of us was clairvoyant." She sighed. "And I wish I knew what has become of poor Miss Willets. We must find her."

A solemn look on his handsome face, he spoke in a gentle voice. "Has it not occurred to you she may have been killed?"

"Of course, it has! But another part of me says it's not too late to save her, and we must do everything in our power to find the lady."

She felt the sweep of his dark eyes. "Anyone would be most fortunate to have you fighting for them."

His comment was as welcome as a hug, even though praise made her uncomfortable. "I possess many shortcomings, but lack of loyalty is not one of them."

"I admire you."

Though she would have preferred he use a different verb, she was nevertheless delighted to have at last earned his admiration. She looked up into his earnest face. "And you have most decidedly won my admiration."

She could tell her compliment made him uncomfortable. "What do we do next?" he asked.

"We must find Miss Willets." Her shoulders sank. "A pity we cannot search the outbuildings."

His gaze on the flames, he was lost in thought for a moment. "She may be here inside Le Chateau."

"What makes you think that?"

"Because there's no reason for either the porters or chair men to wish to harm the woman. So who does that leave?"

"Someone inside Le Chateau."

"And even though you believe Becker is lying, it makes no sense for him to have plotted against the governess."

She nodded. "No. I believe our foul French co-travelers or else the Italian couple—for reasons I cannot possibly conjecture—are responsible for Miss Willets' disappearance."

"It does seem that if the Italians were culpable, there would have been something in their room to show a connection to Miss Willets."

"Yes, that's true. Which points to the dastardly French. Do they not have the inn's entire second level all to themselves?"

"I feel a fool for not having already thought of that."

"It's so very perplexing. The Frenchmen's guilt would be vastly obvious were it not for the fact they were in the eating room when my journal was stolen. We must search the unoccupied rooms on the second level. Perhaps while they're playing cards today."

He shook his head. "We'll search at night when everyone is fast asleep."

She shuddered. "You suggest we attempt to enter their chambers as they sleep?"

"Not that. We need first to eliminate the so-called unoccupied chambers on that floor as potential hiding places for Miss Willets. I'll try to glean from Becker the room numbers of the chambers occupied by the brothers."

She put a hand on his woolen coat sleeve. "Perhaps we should ask the girl with braids instead of Becker. I don't trust the man."

"Why do we not have you ask the girl for the room number of Pierre, and I'll ask Becker for the number of the other brother's room. That way, I believe we can avoid generating suspicion."

"You know their names?"

"I learned them this morning."

How fortunate she was to have been befriended by Lord Stephen Stanhope. "It's a pity we can't do something today to further our inquiries."

"It's best that we wait until they're asleep. Do you play chess?"

"Badly."

"I've brought a traveling chess set. Can I entice you?"

She eked out a smile. "I suppose it will help pass this dreary day."

But throughout that chilling gray day, she could not remove her thoughts from their nighttime quest. She was terrified, terrified of being discovered, terrified of what they might discover.

CHAPTER NINE

T HE ABBREVIATED DAYS and long nights of mid-December
  pushed schedules up. Dinners were served at four-thirty in
the afternoon because it was already night, and all activities
within the Le Chateau drew to a close before ten each night.

This night was no exception. The Frenchmen continued their
habit of playing cards in the eating room until ten, when they
retired to their respective rooms on the second level, and the
Belgians on the third.

Once the Frenchmen started for their chambers, Stephen and
Lady Mary rose, and he swelled with pride as she took his
proffered arm. She looked especially fetching this evening in her
red velvet gown. How could any man at Le Chateau be immune
to her abundant beauty?

He and she were less than a minute behind the Frenchmen as
they climbed the stairs. Stephen observed the Fontaine brothers
both going into Room 1, which he had learned from Becker was
Charles Fontaine's chamber. Pierre slept in Room 3. This was an
unfortunate development.

This would certainly delay the men's bedtime—and conse-
quently, the time when Stephen and Mary could begin their
search of the second level. It also meant that Stephen would have
to contrive a way to know when Pierre returned to his own
chamber.

During the evening, as Stephen and Mary had played chess in the inglenook, they had whispered their plans for the wee hours of the morning. "If the men go to bed at ten, as they do each night," Mary had said, "then I think to be safe from discovery, we should wait until midnight to conduct our search."

It seemed the prudent thing to do.

But how much longer would the brothers stay awake now? How would Stephen even know when Pierre returned to his room? Their chamber walls were so thick, it would be impossible for Stephen to hear when doors opened and closed on the floor below—unless he were not in his chamber. He must stand in the third-floor corridor.

He hated to risk being discovered outside his room, especially by the Italians, who might already suspect him of tampering with their lock. Thankfully, the Italians were always the first to bed, no doubt to implement instructions depicted in their bedside book.

Stephen passed by his own chamber to walk Lady Mary to her door. She paused in front of her door, retrieved her key from her pocket, and then turned to him. Her face lifted, and she began to whisper. "I suppose one of us will have to stay here in the corridor to learn when the brothers will finally separate for the night to get some sleep."

"I will." He flashed a grin and spoke huskily. "I'll position myself between my room and yours so, if caught, it will appear I'm on my way to share my lady's bed."

Candlelight from the nearby wall sconce flickered in her pale eyes as her sultry gaze met his. He did not know if it was the proximity to her bed or her significant appeal that captivated him so thoroughly. All he knew for certain was that acute desire for this woman strummed through him like the very blood in his veins.

Only by the greatest restraint—and the constant memory that she was Devere's cherished sister—was he able to keep from hauling her into his arms, kissing her senseless, and carrying her to that bed.

Were the tables turned, and Devere was here with Stephen's sister, Sarah, Stephen believed Devere would conduct himself as a gentleman. Devere had earned the respect of every man who knew him. When they were youths, Devere had been the almost-worshipped upperclassman to the younger Stephen.

"If he stays long in his brother's chamber," she said, "we may have to push back the time of our search."

He nodded. "I've been thinking . . . there's no reason for you to come. I'll do it alone."

She shook her head adamantly. "No! I must be there in case we find Miss Willets. And even if we don't, I may be able to identify something that belonged to her."

What she said made sense. "I just want to protect you."

Her lovely face softened. "And I appreciate that." She placed a gentle hand on his forearm. He could have groaned from want. "I appreciate you," she whispered. She went to unlock her door, then looked up at him once more. "Tap at my door when you think the time is right. I'll be ready."

SHE HAD CHANGED from her red velvet dinner dress into the black crepe mourning dress she'd begun to wear when Princess Amelia died four years previously and which Mary never traveled without, just in case. Now it would hopefully keep her from being detected in the darkness. Her light locks were covered with a black lace mantilla Sophia had sent her from Spain. Lastly, she donned dark satin slippers that would muffle the sound of footsteps.

During the hours she waited for Stephen's knock, she had thrown two logs on the fire she faced as she read about the Viennese waltz and dreamed of gliding across a dance floor with Lord Stephen Stanhope. He would be the most handsome man there.

One o'clock came, and still Stephen had not knocked. She began to wonder if he'd gone on without her, as he had suggested. Or had Pierre Fontaine's stay in his sibling's chamber lengthened?

When one thirty came and went, she unlocked her chamber door and eased it open. The wall sconces in the corridor had all been snuffed, and it was in complete darkness. A light footfall came closer, and then Stephen stood before her.

"Pierre didn't leave his brother's chamber until midnight. We'd better wait until two."

"As you wish," she murmured.

This time, with Stephen guarding her door, locking her door was unnecessary.

At two, she heard his tap and hurried from her room, locking the door behind her.

"Will you be able to see down the stairs?" he asked in a whisper. "The darkness is total."

"I'll hold on tightly to the banister and take two feet to a step for safety."

"Good. I'll do the same."

He went first.

She had never attempted to descend a staircase without even a hint of light. It was frightening. Her foot hugged the edge of each tread before she slowly lowered to the next as her hands tightly gripped the banister. Descending the dark stairs took more than twice the time it would have with light.

When they reached the second level, what the British refer to as the first floor, they went straight to the first room on the opposite end of the corridor from the brothers as they had previously arranged.

Because it was unoccupied, the room was not locked. Its door squeaked when they eased it open. Her heartbeat drummed. Moonlight shone into the chamber from the window. Because there was no fire, the room was frightfully cold.

It was furnished exactly like her chamber but had no linens on the bed. Given the disregard for cleanliness she'd observed here at the inn, she was surprised they even washed the linens. She looked in the linen press while he peeked under the bed. They found nothing.

The rooms on this level were numbered from 1 to 7. Becker had told Stephen 1 was occupied by Charles Fontaine, and the girl told Mary that Pierre Fontaine was in Number 3.

After the futile search of Room 7, they went to 6. It, too, was unoccupied and unlocked. And it, too, held nothing of interest. The same held for Room 5, then 4. None of them were locked.

How she wished she had worn a cloak! Going into all those frigid chambers was very much like traipsing through the snow in nothing more than her night shift.

And it had all been for naught. None of them contained anything of interest.

"Shall we try Room 2?" he asked in a whisper.

Her stomach tightened queasily. Room 2 was between the Fontaine brothers. Earlier in the day, Stephen and she had noted an added lock secured Room 2. If it made a noise when Stephen attempted to open it, the Frenchmen might awaken and catch them in the commission of their stealthy search.

Clasping the sheathed knife she'd jammed into her pocket, she finally nodded.

How he would manage unfastening the lock with no light, she could not imagine.

"When we first saw the lock this afternoon," he whispered, "I thought it looked just like yours."

"I did, too."

"Let me try your key."

She retrieved it from her pocket and felt in the dark for his outstretched hand.

She could tell from the sound that her key was working. "Now I know how someone got into my chamber," she whispered.

He removed the lock and then eased open the door while she

held her breath. The slightest noise could awaken the men sleeping on either side of this room.

"Quick," he said when the door was halfway open, "get in so we can shut the door."

They hurried into the chamber, which was lightened only from the moonlight streaming in the window. She had hoped to find Miss Willets here, but there was no one. The bed had been made up as if for a guest, and a portmanteau stood in the corner.

She moved to the corner like a cat on soft paws. "Stephen!"

He came to her. "This looks like Miss Willets' portmanteau!"

"Let's see if we can open it." He kneeled down and tried the lock, then looked up, shaking his head. "No luck. It's locked."

It wasn't likely the portmanteau's key would still be in this chamber, but she had to look. She searched on the bedside table and on top of the linen press but found nothing. The linen press was completely empty.

He came to stand beside her.

"It's as if this was supposed to be Miss Willets' room," she said.

His voice was grim when he spoke. "I'm inclined to believe you."

"Miss Willets would have demanded that her room be next to mine. Our rooms were always beside each other's."

"We'll discuss this tomorrow. We need to get out of here now. As quietly as possible."

STEPHEN AND LADY Mary slept later than normal that morning and were the last ones to enter the eating room. Mary made an effort to discuss the events of the previous night over breakfast, but he insisted they wait until they were alone.

By the time they finished their tea and cheeses and egg, along with bread that was stale enough to crack an egg, the Italians had left the chamber and claimed the inglenook.

When he and Lady Mary strode past their favorite meeting spot and realized it was already occupied, Mary looked up at him with a grave face.

He cupped her elbow and steered her to the staircase. "We'll have privacy in one of our rooms."

He took her to his chamber and closed the door behind them. "Pray, won't you sit, my lady?"

She sat on the settee close to the fire. He chose to stand. It wouldn't do to allow himself to be too intimate with the lady. "Looks as if the girl has freshened my fire. I left my locks off and asked her to bring fresh logs this morning."

"She may not clean, but she does make herself useful."

He began to pace the wooden floor. "I owe you an apology, my lady."

She regarded him from beneath lowered brows. "You are now convinced that I did not make up Miss Willets?"

He nodded shamefacedly and went to peer from the window. The porters were once again attempting to dig a path from their quarters to the main house. The snowfall was less intense today than it had been the day before.

"You recall what you said about me being able to command respect from other men?"

"Because you're tall," she said with a nod.

He grinned. "I don't know that I agree with that, but as you must know, being the daughter and sister of an earl, rank does most certainly command respect."

"Indeed. Having a title can be vastly useful. I learned that before I learned to read. I've been able to observe that even an aristocrat with a minor title can render those of lesser rank foolish to gain approval or to claim the slightest intimacy with. But what does this have to do with our situation?"

"I believe that because I'm the son of a powerful duke—even though we're no longer in England—people like Becker are eager to court my favor."

"I do believe that. I see the way the man defers to you."

He spun around to face her. "It's time I confront him with the facts I know and demand an explanation."

Her lovely eyes widened. "He'll just lie."

"I won't accept another lie. I'll insist on the truth."

"But once the no-good, wretched, lying miscreants know that you believe in me, you will no longer be able to move among them with impunity. I, for one, value that you can currently stride both factions."

He gave her a cool look. "And what good has that done us?"

Us? She could almost weep with joy. She had been feeling as if she were trudging alone up a mountain that had no end, and now this gallant knight was lifting her from a crushing gloom. "You're right."

"I'll speak bluntly to Becker now."

CHAPTER TEN

W HY WAS IT whenever Stephen wished to speak to Becker, the man was nowhere to be found? He wasn't in the informal reception area, nor was he in the eating room, where the four men were playing their usual game of whist.

Stephen strode to the door that led to the kitchen, and boldly flung it open. A rotund woman whose gray hair was gathered into a bun at the nape of her neck looked up at him from a mound of dirty plates, a shocked look on her face.

"I'm looking for Mr. Becker," he said in French.

He wasn't sure if she understood French because her only reply was a shrug of her shoulders.

He tried German.

This time she answered. "He may be in his apartments."

Even though Stephen hadn't minded barging into the kitchen, he would feel awkward knocking upon the door to the proprietor's living quarters. He politely excused himself and went to wait near the door to Becker's chambers.

The wait stretched from half an hour to an hour. Finally, Stephen located a crudely fashioned wooden chair and sat on it. Another half-hour passed before the door to Becker's chambers opened, and the innkeeper emerged.

When he saw Stephen, his face brightened. "My lord, may I help you?"

Stephen got to his feet but did not return his host's smile. "There's a matter I need to discuss with you," he said in a grave voice.

Becker's face collapsed. "Is there a problem, my lord?"

The innkeeper always addressed him by *my lord*, as if hosting a member of the aristocracy lent prestige to his establishment.

"Indeed there is." Stephen moved closer and lowered his voice. "Who is supposed to be occupying Room 2?"

At the mention of Room 2, Becker's face blanched. He did not answer for a moment. "No one is in Room 2."

"Then why is there a lock on its door? The other unoccupied chambers are not locked."

Anger flashed in Becker's deep blue eyes. "You've been checking those doors?"

Stephen nodded. "Lady Mary is still looking for her missing friend."

"I know of no such friend," Becker said curtly. "You were not here when Lady Mary arrived. She was . . . how do I say it? Very disoriented."

"She's not disoriented now." Stephen eyed the man sternly. "She still maintains her friend has disappeared."

Becker took a moment to gather his response. "I cannot help you find imaginary people. As to Room 2, the room is not occupied, but it has been paid for." He shrugged. "I suppose it's used for extra storage."

"Who's paying for it?"

Becker's face went grim. "I am bound by professional ethics not to reveal private information about my guests."

Stephen was almost certain the man was void of professional ethics. More likely, his silence had been purchased. "Do you have a key for the lock on Room 2?"

"No. The lock must have been placed there by the person who pays for the chamber."

"Does Le Chateau keep a guest register?" Since Stephen had not signed any such book, he was fairly certain he knew the answer to his question.

Becker's pudgy index finger pointed to his temple. "No need, my lord. I remember all my guests." He tapped his forehead. "Right here."

Stephen considered making inquiries about the suspicious Italian couple, but it was best to concentrate on one matter at a time. Learning who paid for Room 2 was his chief priority at this time. "Remembering the names of all your guests is a remarkable achievement."

A smile on his face, Stephen produced a gold coin and set it on the table that separated the two men.

Becker's gaze dropped to it, then met Stephen's.

"I'm most interested to learn the name of the party who's paying for Room 2," Stephen said.

A muscle twitched in Becker's face, and his voice hardened. "Keep your money."

***

BEFORE STEPHEN BROKE the crushing news to Lady Mary and before Becker had the opportunity to disclose to his co-conspirators that Stephen knew about Room 2, Stephen thought it expedient to further question the Frenchmen.

His Belgian traveling companions had once again joined the French brothers.

The Frenchmen looked up from their game of whist when he entered the eating room and moved to their table. He pulled over a chair and addressed Charles Fontaine, the brother he suspected was the elder. "Do you mind if I watch?"

"Of course not."

Stephen sat and watched as they finished their hand. Then he cleared his throat. "By the way, which of you has paid for Room 2?"

The brothers exchanged surprised looks, and Charles responded, "I don't know what you're talking about."

"I just thought that seeing as that room comes between you two brothers, you must have needed it for extra storage."

Now Pierre spoke. "We know nothing about it."

Though he was not only skeptical but downright disbelieving, Stephen merely smiled and said, "I would have thought that you two would want to be next to each other, and since there are so many unoccupied chambers on your floor, you would have taken, say, Rooms 7 and 6 instead of 1 and 3."

Charles shrugged. "Monsieur Becker must have had his reasons for putting us where he did."

"Oh, well," Stephen said in a casual voice, "I was just curious. I was also curious to know if you men are regular travelers through these mountains. It seems Becker's established a relationship with you as he would with fairly frequent guests."

"We've never before left France," Pierre said, eyeing the brother who so favored him in coloring.

"It's the Italians who come here on a regular basis," Charles offered.

"Do you mean that they come here as a stop while traveling, or could they possibly choose to come here for a holiday?"

"It's my impression they choose to holiday here." Charles shook his head in mock disbelief. "Crazy, if you ask me."

"Who would choose to freeze their bum off for a holiday?" Pierre asked, laughing heartily at his own comment, revealing crooked, discolored teeth.

Stephen took the opportunity to study their clothing. Nothing about their dress or tailoring indicated they would merit any kind of position at the Congress at Vienna. Their jackets were ill fitting and of inferior fabric, not to mention that they looked as if they had seen several years of use. Their cravats looked as if they'd neither been washed nor ironed in weeks, and the soles on their boots were wearing thin. By contrast, the Belgians who'd traveled with Stephen dressed as gentlemen of means.

As Stephen sat there observing the Frenchmen, he came to

the conclusion he needed to get into the brothers' chambers. He felt certain he would find Lady Mary's journal—if not Miss Willets herself. For he had definitely come to believe in the woman's existence.

He especially hoped—for Lady Mary's sake—he wouldn't find Miss Willets' remains.

But how could he gain entrance? Becker had proven he would not be of use. There was also the fact the men had brought their own locks. Even if Stephen were able to coax the girl with braids to help, she would not be able to get past the men's locks.

A tall ladder could allow him to enter through their windows, none of which were locked, but there was no way Stephen would be able to acquire and use a ladder without being seen. And it would still be some time before the depth of snow could be reduced enough for Stephen to even search the outbuildings for a ladder.

His thoughts turned to the Italian couple. Since they were here when Lady Mary arrived, they might have seen Miss Willets. He needed to speak to them. A pity they spent so much time in their chamber—or likely more accurately, their bed.

After an hour, he took his leave from the card players, thinking he would find the Italians in the inglenook, but they were not there. He then climbed the stairs to Lady Mary's chamber and tapped at the door to share with her his grim news.

"I TOLD YOU that dishonest, deceitful, thoroughly miscreant innkeeper would lie," Mary responded when Lord Stephen told her about his encounter with Becker. "But I am surprised the deviant wasn't enticed by your gold. I'm certain he's already sold himself once since I arrived here."

"I agree."

As angry as she was, there was a huge measure of comfort in

having Lord Stephen as her ally. And truth be told, every time she looked at him, her heartbeat quickened. Having him—all six feet plus of him—standing here in the intimacy of her bedchamber made her feel like a heap of butter melting in front of the fire.

It was difficult to concentrate on her nightmarish predicament when he was so close, but she must.

His black eyes held hers. She sighed. "I am rather wealthy in my own right. Perhaps I could offer a heftier bribe to the wretched man."

"It may have to come to that but, at present, I'm so out of charity with Becker, it makes me sick to think of him profiting from your ill use."

It was all she could do not to throw herself into Lord Stephen's arms with gratitude and something else . . . love.

Love? Her breath stilled. Yes, she was quite sure the reason she'd never accepted any of those proposals of marriage was because none of them had come from Lord Stephen Stanhope.

In every way, Stephen had proven to be her rescuing knight. But even if he hadn't, she resoundingly knew this was the only man upon whom she could ever bestow her affections.

He embodied the most important qualities a prospective husband could possess. His fine appearance aside, he was caring, clever, and moved within the same social circles as her family.

Lord Stephen Stanhope was a giant of a man—and not just in physical stature. Everything about him bespoke power, especially the self-assured manner in which he alone stood against other men. What bravery he had displayed by taking her side in opposition to all these men at Le Chateau. She greatly admired anyone who championed the friendless, especially when she was the one who was friendless.

And it wasn't just she who was impressed by this man's abundant charms. Over the past several years, their country had entrusted him with important duties because he had pointedly established his worth.

How could she not have fallen in love with him?

Though he had been kind to her and protective of her, he had never in any way shown that he was attracted to her as a man is to a woman—not even this morning when he'd asked her into his bedchamber.

She prayed she could awaken in him the same intense feelings he had ignited in her. She could not, though, allow him to think her a doxy. Instead of swooning over him now, she needed to gather her wits. "I daresay it will be vastly interesting to see what you can learn from the Italians—if you can ever get them alone. What in the wide world is it they find to do in their bedchamber for so many hours each day?"

His eyes flashed with what she could only perceive as humor, and he gave a little cough. "Perhaps they're just reticent because of the supposed language barrier."

"To quote you, dear sir, *there is that.*"

He chuckled.

He had not taken a seat in her chamber, though she had invited him to. Now he strode to the door. "I have correspondence I should address." Then he stopped and turned back. "However, the inglenook's unoccupied if you'd care to come play a game of chess with me."

"Oh, yes, please. You will be saving me from leaping from my chamber window to relieve the boredom."

"I believe the lady does embellish a bit."

With a pensive stare, she met his gaze. "Only in jest. I vow to be always honest with you, my dear Lord Stephen."

THAT NIGHT, MARY went to her chamber at the usual time, just past ten o'clock. She was pleased to find that her fire—a quite hearty one—had just been built up, and additional logs had been neatly stacked beside it. She had given her key to the braided blonde for just such a purpose.

Before today, she could never have entrusted her key to anyone other than Lord Stephen, but since she had brought no jewels and since her journal had been stolen, she knew none of her possessions would be of interest to anyone here. That was not to say she would not continue to lock her chamber at all times.

The room had already become toasty warm. For one like she who was accustomed to being assisted by a lady's maid, removing her clothing was difficult, but she managed. Then, dressed in a warm flannel night shift, she climbed upon her tall feather bed and pulled the eiderdown over her.

Once she snuffed her candle, though, she found herself resistant to sleep. Her mind was too full. Only this night, she was not contemplating Miss Willets and the conspiracy to wipe out the old woman's existence.

This night, all Mary's thoughts were on Stephen. Sophia had certainly been right when she'd told Mary she would know when she met THE one. It was such an exhilarating feeling to experience the heady intoxication of falling in love. Nothing in her previous one-and-twenty years could have prepared her for this onslaught of powerful emotions.

Just lying there thinking of him, picturing his penetrating black eyes and wry grin spreading over his chiseled face, sent a thumping to her chest and molten heat centering low in her torso.

She was in a quandary as to how she should act on these newly discovered feelings. Should she flirt? Should she cast away her pride and admit to him her love? Or should she act the perfect lady and wait for him to show some sign that she was more to him than a damsel in distress?

She lay there for at least three hours, thinking of this man she loved. She tried to recall every conversation they'd shared, tried to remember if he'd ever in any way shown her that he could be falling in love with her. But there was nothing to indicate that he'd done so.

What if he was already spoken for? What if he was in love

with another woman?

As painful as it would be to let this paragon slip away, Lady Mary Beresford was possessed of far too much pride to humiliate herself over this man, no matter how thoroughly she adored him and everything about him.

With that admission, she finally drifted off to sleep.

In her dream, she was having difficulty breathing. It was almost as if she were being smothered.

Then she realized this was not a dream.

Someone's trying to kill me!

She tried to fling off the pillow crushing into her face, but her strength was no match for her attacker's. It had to be a man.

Panic seized her. She tried to gasp for breath, but it was as futile as penetrating steel with a feather.

Her attempt to open her eyes was futile. There was nothing but darkness. A pillow was being pushed down over her face. She tried to fling it off but she was not strong enough.

She was going to die. In spite of her pure panic, she recalled what Devere had told her to do if ever she was threatened. "There's not a man alive who could continue an assault if you kick or knee him in the groin as hard as you can."

How could she manage that when she was deprived of her vision? He had not been able to steal the use of her hands. She thought he was on her right, and she reached out to confirm.

Struggling for breath, she had to act fast even though she was greatly handicapped without sight or hearing.

Disabling him was her only hope. Either try or die. First, though, she had to free her legs of the heavy eiderdown.

Because her attacker was not prepared for that, she was able to kick away her covers. She whisked up her ankle-length shift to give her legs a wider range.

She had to make her best guess as to where she must place her knee thrust. She couldn't breathe. She had to act quickly. As hard as she could, she drove her knee into his groin.

His guttural groan told her she had succeeded. Then she was

easily able to fling off the pillow. A darkly clothed man writhed at her side. She could not identify him for he wore a black hood.

She screamed as loud as her lungs would allow, and the would-be killer fled her chamber.

She shook all over as she scurried from her bed in pursuit, then she stopped. What if he had a knife? She must get her own knife.

In the dark corridor a moment later, gripping her knife, she saw nothing, heard nothing. He'd vanished as surely as Miss Willets.

Weeping now, she pounded on Stephen's door.

CHAPTER ELEVEN

S TEPHEN WAS IN so deep a sleep that the knock on his door fed into his fuzzy dream where the tapping transitioned to a steady rattle of wheels upon a cobbled street in a city he thought was Vienna. It was a moment before he became cognizant that the incessant pounding was actually on his door. *At Le Chateau.*

What the devil? What the bloody time was it? Who would be calling on him in the middle of the night? He reluctantly climbed from the warmth of his bed, found his jacket, and threw it on. He started for the door, then stopped. What if the knocker was an armed man?

He went back to his bedside table and grabbed his knife before crossing the chamber, undoing his locks, and slowly easing open the door.

Even though the corridor was as dark as the inside of a well, he knew the whimpering person standing there was Lady Mary. She flung herself into his arms and burst into tears. He hauled her into his chamber.

Before he could hold her properly, he dropped his knife on the top of the linen press. Then with both arms, he drew her trembling body close. The feel of her was much to his liking, but he could not consider his own feelings while such misery possessed her. "What's happened?" he asked, his voice tender.

Her slender shoulders shook as she strove to draw in her

breath. He traced soothing circles on her back and murmured, "You're all right now."

She sniffed. "Please lock the door."

With disappointment, he withdrew from her and secured his lock. He then lighted a candle and looked at the upset young beauty. His pulse quickened when he saw that she wore a night shift. Even though he already knew she was extremely upset, the proof of her distress in the rivulets of tears that still slid down her delicate face, in the way her body shook, and in the sheer terror in her shifting, reddened eyes made him determined to do anything to bring back the flippant Lady Mary he'd come to know.

He came and put a reassuring arm around her and spoke softly. "Now, tell me what's happened."

"Someone . . ." She burst into a fresh round of tears that wracked her whole body.

He drew her closer, patting her shoulders. Then it occurred to him that someone must have come into her bedchamber as she slept. "Dear God, did someone enter your chamber?" He held her at arm's length and peered at her.

Her eyes were red, and her face was slick with the tears that flowed as if from a spigot. She nodded. "He tried to kill me."

He closed his eyes from revulsion. "I failed you. We knew they had a key to your room. I should have done something."

"It's not your fault."

But he could have prevented this. She could be dead right now. He was furious with himself. He should at least have given her his locks. He was far better equipped to fend off a would-be killer than this slightly built female. But who would ever have thought someone would try to kill her? "Tell me everything that happened."

She collapsed against him and clung like heated wax until her crying eventually tapered off. "I awakened to find someone pushing a pillow into my face."

It sickened him to think that this could have happened—and right next to his chamber. She would not have been able to see anything, nor could she even scream to summon him. Thank God she had survived. "How were you able to fight off such an attack?"

"I owe my survival to Devere."

His brows lowered. "How is that possible?"

"He instructed his sisters of a particular thrust he said would disable any attacker, and he proved to be right."

Smirking, Stephen nodded knowingly. His admiration for Devere increased even more. A pity he had given her brother his word that he'd not reveal their acquaintance. "I understand. Bravo to you—and to Devere. Would that you could have done to him what he wanted to do to you."

"You mean kill him?"

Stephen was not normally so bloodthirsty, but he would have had no qualms about killing a fiend who tried to murder a sleeping woman. "He deserves it."

"He most certainly does, the beastly, no-good, murdering spawn of Lucifer."

Stephen sighed. It was good to have Mary back. Thanks to Devere. Would she ever know how much she owed her brother? Had it not been for Devere, she would have been completely alone in this evil place. "So when you disabled him, did you not see him well enough to identify him?"

She shook her head forlornly. "It was a male, and he wore a dark hood. I tried to follow him, but it was as if he had vanished. I saw nothing, heard nothing."

"You went right after him?" asked Stephen, his brows lowered.

"Not exactly. I started to, but then I went back and got my knife. By the time I reached the corridor, there was no evidence of him. He'd completely vanished, like Miss Willets."

"You had to have heard footsteps."

"I would have, had I not made the mistake of going back for my knife."

"No. You did the right thing. It was not worth risking your

life to identify him. Had you confronted him in the corridor, he could very well have tried to finish the job he started, only with a knife."

She winced. "I can see why he preferred smothering me—to make it look like a natural death."

He eased away from her. Holding her felt entirely too good. He had to keep reminding himself this was Devere's little sister. "Especially since it's been established you were sick when you arrived here. They all would have brushed off your demise by saying you suffered from poor health."

She gave a mock groan. "And they would just have dumped my cold, dead body into the snow," she said with a martyred expression.

"This is no teasing matter. Were it not for your brother, you most likely would be dead right now."

"Too true. I couldn't even call out with that instrument of murder smashing into my face."

"It sickens me to think I wouldn't have been able to help you." The fire in his hearth was on the verge of going out, so he moved away from her and stooped to throw a pair of logs and some kindling onto it. After he succeeded in building up the fire, he beckoned for her to come sit close to it on the settle. "You must be cold in just your night shift. Shall I go to your room to fetch a shawl or something?"

She whipped around to face him, terror in her eyes. "No, please, don't leave me!"

How thoughtless of him. Of course, after what she'd been through she would quite naturally be terrified of being left alone again. "Forgive my thoughtlessness." He moved to his portmanteau and procured a black velvet jacket which he placed over her shoulders.

It was only then he realized what a ridiculous sight he was in his own long night shirt topped by a brass-buttoned coat. "I must also beg your forgiveness for my state of undress."

"I come barging into your room in the middle of the night,

and you beg my forgiveness?"

"There is that," he said with a smile and a shrug.

His comment coaxed a smile from her.

He was in a quandary as to whether he should don proper clothing or just continue on in his night clothes. Dressing in the same chamber that she occupied, he reasoned, would be more embarrassing to a maiden. Even an unconventional maiden like Lady Mary Beresford.

He thought of sitting beside her on the settee but discarded such a notion. It would have been far too intimate a gesture while both of them wore night clothing. Instead he pulled up a crudely fashioned wooden chair.

"I am supremely grateful you believe me. About my attacker."

"One cannot fake the kind of terror you demonstrated."

"There is that," she said with little laugh.

It pleased him that a calmness was replacing her anguish. "The attempt on your life is testament to the fact you're upsetting the person or persons responsible for Miss Willets' disappearance."

"They're likely upset because they now know you must believe me."

He nodded. "Becker has told him or them about my inquiries."

"I am, like you, inclined to believe the French brothers must be responsible for Miss Willets' . . . loss—though I'm perplexed over the theft of my journal. I know they couldn't have stolen it."

"I'm inclined to believe they have an accomplice, and Becker is the only possible candidate."

It was obvious Mary hated to use the word *death* in connection with the aged governess, even though it seemed improbable the woman could still be alive. But why in the devil would someone wish to kill a harmless old governess?

"That empty room does point to them," he said. "That and the fact they're not who they claim to be. I would wager everything I possess that those men are in no way connected to the Congress of Vienna."

"I had noticed they dress remarkably shabby for ones who claim such a connection."

He nodded.

"The question now is, do we notify Becker of the murder attempt? For all we know, he could have been the culprit," she said.

"I'm not ruling Becker out, but there's no question whatsoever that we *will* tell everyone a murderer lurks in the very building in which we're sleeping."

She heaved a sigh. "So now *I'm* a threat to them. Miss Willets and I. But why?"

"You're a threat because you know someone at Le Chateau is responsible for Miss Willets' disappearance." He shrugged. "Why she was a threat is a mystery."

Her eyes sparkled. "Do you suppose that instead of a governess she was actually a jewel thief? Perhaps after ingratiating herself with her wealthy employers, she sneaked into their chambers and stole valuable jewels. Perhaps these cutthroats at Le Chateau followed her in order to take back the jewelry."

Lady Mary was certainly possessed of a lively imagination. "Such a scenario is possible—as is your supposition about her being a royal-switched-at-birth or some such concoction."

She folded her arms across her chest and eyed him with amusement even though it was obvious her hands were still shaking from her recent ordeal. "In other words, you're saying it's anyone's guess?"

He nodded.

Her shoulders sagged. "Truth be told, if you ever saw sweet little Miss Willets, you would never be able to believe her a jewel thief. A more innocuous-looking elder woman never existed."

There must be something in the woman's history to explain her mysterious disappearance. "I want to know everything you can possibly remember about her. I remember you saying she was from Oxford, she'd been a governess to French children for decades, the children at her last family grew up, and her new employer is something big at the Congress of Vienna. But there must be more you can tell me."

"She was a wee bit smaller than me. She wore spectacles. Her hair was silver."

He nodded. "And she played cards."

"Yes. She loaned her cards to those dreadful devils because she preferred my companionship over playing games. She enjoyed sitting before the fire with me and just reminiscing about England and asking about my family."

"Do you know the name of the important Frenchman in Vienna who employed her?"

She pursed her mouth. "I know she told me, but I cannot recall."

"And I'd come to believe you possessed of an excellent memory."

"I usually do recall rather well. Perhaps if I truly concentrate on it, I shall remember. Don't speak for a moment. It might come." She stared at the fire for a considerable period of time. "I've got it! Monsieur d'Arblay! I remember it because it was the same name as Fanny Burney's husband."

"The authoress? I didn't know she married."

"She was quite the confirmed spinster when she finally married a French refugee. She must have been forty."

"If there is a Monsieur d'Arblay representing France at the Congress, it will give validity to the lady's identity, and it will be easy enough to prove. I've been studying hundreds of pages of documents relating to the Congress, and I've a list of all the attendees."

He moved to his portmanteau and procured a large pouch of papers. After going through them for a few moments he located the list. The list of Frenchmen was short. Her read over it, and then looked up at her. "There is no d'Arblay."

"I cannot believe that sweet little woman would lie to me!"

"She apparently was not whom she claimed to be."

"So there is an alternative explanation of who she really is?"

"I believe so, but how are we to learn her identity? You said she showed no signs of wealth?"

"No—other than the fine coach she said her employer had sent for her."

"Which was probably a lie."

"She dressed exactly like a governess . . . wait! There was one thing . . . she wore the most divine furry boots. They were very costly—which she explained by saying her last employer provided them for his entire staff. She said they were only available in the little French mountain village where the family's country chateau was located. According to her story—which I don't know if I can believe now—an elderly farmer fashioned them during the winter months."

His brows lowered. "What did they look like?"

She held up her own bare foot. "Well, her feet were small like mine. The boots went halfway up the calf and were constructed entirely of some kind of soft brown fur. The only fur I recognize is ermine. This fur was less expensive, more common than ermine."

"I've seen the boots."

Her eyes widened, her mouth gaped open. "Where?"

"In the Italians' chamber."

"Dear Lord! Do you think they killed her for her boots?"

"I doubt they'd be worth killing for, but it does rather point to their potential guilt."

"I will demand an explanation tomorrow!"

"No, I will. You've put yourself in harm's way enough already."

Her shoulders sank. "I don't know what I would have done without you, my noble knight."

If only she knew she had her brother—not him—to thank. "And one thing more . . ."

"What?" She had never looked so fragile as she did at that

moment with the firelight simmering in her remarkable eyes, her hair tussled. Tonight in her bare feet and skimpy night shift she looked almost childlike, certainly helpless.

He had never felt more committed to fulfilling a duty than he did now. How right Devere had been to fear for his youthful sister. "You're to sleep in my chamber from now on."

Chapter Twelve

He wants me to share his bed? His comment stunned her. Then she realized he wasn't interested in sleeping with her. He wanted only to protect her. While she was gratified that he cared for her safety, she was mildly disappointed he did not look upon her romantically.

Because she was so shaken from the attack, she yearned to be taken in his powerful arms, to feel the steady thump of his heart beneath her ear, to be swaddled in his love. She needed him for her very existence in the same way that fire blazing in his hearth needed wood. She wanted more than his protection. She craved his love.

No matter how feverishly she desired him, she refused to be the aggressor. She could not afford to destroy her reputation. She'd gone down that perilous road once before and vowed to never succumb again.

Also, she refused to beg for feelings he could not reciprocate.

"I vow I will be a gentleman." He watched her with an earnest expression.

She eyed the bed. It would be a squeeze, but the bed was large enough for two. It would have to be since there was nowhere else in the chamber to sleep. Unless . . .

"I can sleep on the settle," she offered. "You're much too large to fold yourself up on it."

"I will own, you're small, but I cannot in good conscience permit a lady to sleep on that wooden settle. It's far too uncomfortable."

"It doesn't signify," she said with a shrug. "At least in here I'll feel safe."

"That's what matters most, but still I cannot allow you to sleep there. For one thing, we have no additional bedding, and it's far too cold to sleep without the benefit of eiderdown."

He was right. He usually was. "Since you've vowed to be a gentleman, I suppose we could share the bed." Before Sophia married, Mary was accustomed to frequently sharing a bed with her sister.

He sucked in his breath, and it was a moment before he responded. "The others have to believe we've become lovers, but I would never compromise a maiden."

His gallantry only made her love him all the more. "Yes, that would not only explain me moving into your chamber, but it will also serve as warning to the would-be murderer not to try again to kill me." A smile eased across her face. "I've a big, strong man to thwart any future attacks against my person."

"I don't know about the big and strong, but I won't allow anyone to harm you, Lady Mary."

"Do you not think that since we're going to be sharing a small bedchamber that you can dispense with the Lady and just call me Mary?"

He regarded her with those mesmerizing dark eyes. "Very well. Would you object to calling me Stephen?"

"It would answer very well." The thought of referring to him so intimately made her quiver even more.

"It will be difficult to maintain privacy in such close quarters," he said. "When it's daylight, and you feel safer, we can move some of your things into this room. But for now, you need to get some sleep."

"I don't know if I can calm down enough to sleep. My heart keeps racing, and my mind is colossally jumbled."

He came to stand behind her and placed his hands on her shoulders. "Please don't worry any more. You're safe now."

His touch soothed her. It was as if his subtle action began to erase her worries. Not conscious of what she was doing, she reached to stroke the back of his hand and sighed.

He abruptly withdrew his hands from her shoulders. "Well, now, shall we turn in? If I thought there was any way I could fit onto that settle, I would, but you'll have to put up with me next to you. I hope my snoring doesn't disturb you."

She didn't think she'd ever heard anyone snore before. "The way I feel right now, any minor annoyance is immensely offset by the comfort of your presence."

"I don't believe another soul could have a key to my lock. The Foreign Office furnishes its diplomats and spies with unique equipment."

Her eyes widened. "Do you know any real spies?"

"Working with spies falls under my duties."

"I won't pry any further, but I think it's terribly fascinating."

"It's not really." He retrieved his knife from the top of the linen press and moved toward the side of the bed closest to the door. "In the unlikely event someone intrudes, I'll be ready." He placed his knife on the bedside table.

She moved to the other side of the bed and climbed atop it. What if she snored? What if she slept with her mouth gaping open like some demented street beggar? Oh, dear, she most sincerely hoped she wouldn't do something that would repel this most wonderful paragon of a man.

He blew out the candle and climbed on the bed. It sank considerably under his weight—so much so, she felt almost as if she could roll down into him. Which she would not object to in the least.

She presented her back to him. That way, if she did sleep like a demented street beggar, he might not see her.

After the candle was extinguished, the chamber was still faintly lit from the lone window. She was comforted that she wasn't in total darkness, that their chamber was warmed by the blazing fire that filled the room with warmth and her lungs with its pungent smell. Most of all, she was comforted that that Stephen lay next to her.

Before long, his breathing changed so dramatically she knew he was asleep. She recalled her mother, who suffered from insomnia, complaining that it was grossly unfair that Papa would fall into a deep sleep the moment his head hit the pillow while poor Mama would toss and turn for hours. Mama claimed it was women, not the men, who shouldered the cares of the world.

Perhaps Mama was right.

In spite of feeling completely safe because of Stephen's commanding proximity, she could not purge her mind of everything she remembered from the vicious, premeditated attack. Some thoroughly evil person intentionally tried to deprive her of life. Over and over, she tied to force herself to recall something from the flashing glimpse she'd gotten of the writhing, hooded man that would help her identify him, but because he was mostly bent over, she was unable to tell either the attacker's height or build, and she didn't see his face at all. There was also the fact that, except for Stephen, the rest of the men under this roof were all of the same height, give or take an inch.

Some person or persons wanted to keep her silent about Miss Willets. Did that mean they had done to Miss Willets what they wanted to do to Mary? Her stomach thudded like one dropping from great height.

Was her attacker acting on his own? Or, as she and Stephen had both suspected, was her attack the concoction of the French brothers?

Now there was a new kink in the conundrum. Why did the Italian woman have Miss Willets' furry boots? Mary simply must see them.

As her mind was beginning to settle, her thoughts gave way to the slumbering man beside her. It felt so natural to call him by his Christian name, as indeed she had begun to think of him that way, and it felt so natural to be lying here with this man she loved.

Her worries began to give way to thoughts of her future. Nothing would give her more pleasure than to be able to sleep beside this man for all the nights of her life.

Could he ever feel that way about her? That he had never made even a remotely romantic gesture toward her rather convinced her he wasn't attracted to women of her ilk. Of course she would not be to his liking. A man possessed of all the fine attributes of Lord Stephen Stanhope could win the heart of any woman. He would court women far more demure than she. She was well aware of her own flamboyant nature, her propensity to speak in hyperbole, her impetuousness, and her sometimes most unladylike behavior. He would most certainly disapprove of a woman who gallivanted about Europe without even a lady's maid.

Somehow, before she drifted off to sleep, she found herself facing him and thinking how fortunate was the woman he would honor with his love. And with his name.

THE FOLLOWING MORNING, Stephen awakened first and allowed himself the luxury of watching her lovely face as she slept. He wondered what she would have looked like in nightwear which would have displayed more of her ivory flesh. A pity it was so wretchedly cold here.

Perhaps it wasn't a pity, after all. Nothing would be served by torturing himself with the temptation of her. It had been difficult enough to lie beside this desirable woman and not wish to draw her into his arms and make love to her, but Devere kept intruding on his thoughts.

Out of respect for his slightly older Oxford chum, he would not permit himself to act upon his own carnal desires.

Nor would he wish to sully the reputation of Lady Mary Beresford. She had come to mean too much to him. They were two disparate English aristocrats thrown together by bizarre circumstances who had forged an impermeable bond.

While Devere had been the link between them, Stephen thought that even without Devere's encouragement, he would have championed Mary against the deviants now inhabiting Le Chateau. *Mary.* Calling her Mary seemed as natural as addressing his sister.

But it was altogether different.

He quietly eased from the bed and began to dress.

The movement must have awakened her. She began to stir. "Good morning, my lady. It's light enough now that we can begin moving your things into my chamber with no fears for your safety."

She sprang up, fear flashing across her face. "You're going to leave me?"

He stepped closer and spoke as he would to a frightened child. "Not if it upsets you. We can go together, or I can leave both doors open."

"You must think me a positive ninny."

"I do not. You were almost murdered last night. Anyone who's been through what you've been through would quite naturally still be terrified. Now just stay in bed while I build up the fire. You don't need to add lung fever to your other woes."

She favored him with a smile.

The fire had not gone out, so he merely added kindling and tossed two more logs on the existing fire and, soon, its heat was filling every corner of the small chamber.

He completed dressing by donning his boots and cursing his lack of a valet, but he could not permit Humphrey in the same bedchamber with the maiden Mary.

Once he was presentable, he stood and faced her, ready to challenge anyone at Le Chateau. "What is my lady's pleasure?"

"I'd rather not traipse about the corridor, even for just a brief

LADY MARY'S DANGEROUS ENCOUNTER

moment, in my night clothes."

He nodded. "So I'll leave both doors open. It shouldn't take me more than a moment to fetch, what? A portmanteau and a valise?"

A sheepish look crossed her face. "I'm epically embarrassed for you to see how untidy my bedchamber is. I daresay I've got possessions strewn all about my room like the messiest hausfrau imaginable."

He chuckled. "It sounds as if you're describing my sisters."

Her brows elevated. "You have sisters in addition to three elder brothers? I haven't heard you speak of them before."

"I have three sisters, and all but one, the youngest, have long been married."

"And the youngest? How old is she? Oh, wait! I do know her! Lady Sarah Stanhope. She came out the year before me. I can't believe I did not realize sooner that lady was your sister. I only barely know her. It's my understanding she spends a great deal of time in the country."

"Yes, my sister is horse mad and always happiest at Halton Court. We fear she's eliminating herself from the Marriage Mart by such actions."

"Lady Sarah will have no difficulty finding a husband. She's lovely—and there is the fact she's a duke's daughter."

"A rather impoverished duke, sad to say."

"The size of her dowry will not signify. Men will be honored to earn her hand in marriage. I daresay she is rather like Sophia and me. Recall that Sophia did not marry until she was seven-and-twenty. We Beresfords are too particular to just settle for a husband. We have most exacting standards. And, as you know, Sophia did very well by waiting. She is ecstatically happy with her handsome scion of England's richest family."

"It hardly seems fair. The Deveres were already one of the wealthiest noble houses in Britain."

"It does rather seem unfair, but I must tell you when Sophia fell in love with William, she had no idea of his true identity, nor did he know hers. It's quite a romantic, adventuresome tale I shall have to tell you some day."

Some day. He wondered if there would ever be a some day in their future when he and she would be together sharing stories. With those intending to do her harm, right now he just prayed they would make it to Vienna.

He watched her as she sat propped up on pillows in *his* bed. The man who would eventually win her hand would be most fortunate, most fortunate indeed—even if she was maddening.

In his thirty years, Stephen had never awakened to having a beautiful maiden of good birth in his bed. But, then, he'd never before had a *maiden* in his bed. It was a novel experience, to be sure.

"Will you permit me to go get your things now?" he asked.

She laughed. "That's jolly, you asking me for permission when you're the bravest, most steadfast man I've ever known. Except for Devere. I am completely in your debt and would bow to your every demand."

He leveled a stern gaze. "I'm not the demanding sort."

"Actually, I'd prefer you just tote the portmanteau here. I shan't wish you to gape at the ravages of my untidiness. Once I'm properly dressed, I shall gather up my own mess, stuff it in my valise, and return to your chamber. I am confident no one will attempt to murder me in daylight." She cast a demure look at him. "And I've you to protect me."

He felt as if he'd grown another inch. He only hoped he could live up to her expectations. He had to keep her safe.

"I say! Would it embarrass you if my man collected your things?

"Not at all. I am accustomed to servants seeing how vastly messy I am."

As if on cue, there was a tap on his door, and there stood Humphrey. "My lord dressed himself?" he asked, shock registering on his face.

Stephen cleared his throat. "As it happens, there's a lady in my chamber. Be a good man and fetch her things from the chamber next door." He tilted his head to the left.

Once Humphrey brought the portmanteau to the room they would be sharing, he said, "I'll just stand out in the corridor while you dress."

In the corridor, which was now fairly well lit, he wondered if it would take her an hour to dress and do her toilette, which was the custom with his sisters. He marveled that she'd come so far without the benefit of her lady's maid. Lady Mary Beresford was a most singular woman, to be sure.

In less than ten minutes, she swung open the door. "We need to talk."

CHAPTER THIRTEEN

H E LAZILY PERUSED her from her freshly swept up coif and sparkling eyes down along the lines of the lace-trimmed seafoam velvet gown that draped the sweet curves of her slight body. How had she managed in just ten minutes to look as if she'd spent an entire morning being preened and primped to perfection?

"My lady looks lovely."

"You're too kind." She swept open the door and went to sit on the settle in front of the fire, patting the space next to her. She obviously wanted him to sit there.

Since they were both now respectably dressed, he complied, his appreciative gaze drawn to the fire. He was rather pleased with the fine job he'd done building it. Such a service was customarily performed by his personal servants. He found it was quite remarkable that she and he, both of whom had been raised among a high degree of privilege, had so well mastered coping on their own. He'd even managed to tie his own cravat that morning. Not well, though.

"I had many things on my mind last night—after you so promptly went to sleep," she chided, her voice light. "And I've decided perhaps we should not disclose to everyone here at Le Chateau that I was the target of a murderous attack."

He whirled to face her. "What would be served by such an

omission?"

"I fear it will only reinforce everyone's opinion that I'm mentally unhinged. Remember, no one else observed the murder attempt." Her voice splintered. "They will never believe me."

It angered him that she was likely right. It had seemed spectacularly right that everyone here be informed that a murderer lurked in their presence. He'd also wanted to put the vile man on alert that he knew all about the thwarted attack on an innocent sleeping woman. He'd wanted that person to know that, in him, Mary had a protector, and he would prevent—even if it cost his own life—any future attempt on her life.

He drew a deep breath. "As much as I hate it, I concede to your judgment, my lady."

"Our next decision is to consider how I can arrange to see those boots in the Italians' chamber."

A pity his description of the boots wasn't sufficient to identify them. Only Mary could say with certainty that they were the ones which had belonged to Miss Willets. Women were like that—able to discern the tiniest detail when it came to matters of fashion. "You, of course, would have to see them yourself. Therefore, we need to think of some way I can keep them engaged while you search their chamber." He hoped the maiden Mary did not come across that particular bedside book when she went to the room they shared. "You will need to be quick."

She nodded thoughtfully. "It's fortuitous that you can speak Italian. Are you fluent?"

"I am."

"My brother Devere is, too. Why is it you fellows all have the opportunity to acquire so much knowledge to which we women have no access? I had begged Papa to permit me to study with a tutor of German, but Papa said it wouldn't be proper for a young lady to be alone in such a manner with male tutor. My dear father would no doubt have apoplexy if he could see me now—were he still alive."

Her face sombered for a moment before she continued.

"Why do you think it is that all the language tutors, except for the French, are men? I so wanted to speak in that Teutonic tongue that is so familiar to our Royal Family."

He regarded her with a bemused expression. "Are you not getting away from the topic we were discussing?"

Her brows lowered and her lips pursed. "Oh, dear. What topic were we discussing? I daresay, my mind flits far too fast."

Indeed, it did. "We were discussing how I might be able to divert the Italians while you break into their chamber."

"Oh, yes." She sat silently for a few moments.

As proud as he'd been of the fire, he thought it too hot when they sat so too close to it. Her face was already flushed from the heat.

"I know," she finally said, "you can claim you're on your way to Italy and need to consult them for recommendations of cities and antiquities to visit."

"That might just answer."

⋙⋘

STEPHEN HAD TOLD her of his difficulties with the Italians' lock, and after much consideration, he told her he knew why he had not succeeded with it. At this point, she honestly didn't care if any of these evil people knew their rooms were being searched—as long as she wasn't caught in the process.

After they had hurriedly eaten breakfast, Stephen had left her at the table while he approached the Italians who, like the others, sat at the same table for each meal. Unlike the others, the Italians' table was against the back wall, far removed from their fellow guests.

Stephen had told her to leave the eating room as soon as she was able to determine he'd been successful in engaging the couple in conversation. When she saw him pull up a chair at their table and the lady smiling broadly at Stephen, Mary quickly left the chamber and managed to scurry up the stairs without being observed.

Stephen had given her a key-like tool to use on the locks.

She knew no other guests would be on the third level because all of them had still been in the eating room when she left. Still, she worried someone would catch her. Her first try at the lock failed. Perspiration slickened her hands, and her pulse accelerated. She tried to recall everything Stephen had told her to do in order to open the lock.

When her second try succeeded, she blew out a grateful breath, flipped off the lock, and hurried into the chamber as if she were trying to outrun an avalanche while managing to quietly close the door behind her.

Her heartbeat racing, she stood inside the room that was so similar to her own and surveyed it. The white-curtained window was in the same place near the fireplace as the one in Stephen's chamber. The bed was larger than the ones in Stephen's room or hers. Her gaze latched on a wood and green leather portmanteau which she instantly recognized as being the woman's because it stood open to reveal two or three changes of feminine clothing.

There at the trunk's bottom stood a pair of lady's boots. There was no doubt in Mary's mind. Those furry boots were same ones that fit Miss Willets' tiny feet. Seeing them brought only a deep sense of loss.

She quickly removed her left half boot and slid her foot into the boot that appeared to be Miss Willets'. It fit perfectly.

She had discovered what she'd come for. There was no need to linger and risk being found where she did not belong.

She quickly put her own boot back on, fled the chamber, and managed to restore the lock and was fairly confident she had secured it. Which was a good thing since she heard steps coming nearer on the staircase. She did not want to be caught here, so she raced to her former chamber, and hurriedly unlocked it. She would have gone into Stephen's chamber had she not observed him securing his private locks when they went to breakfast. Its key safely rested in his pocket.

Locked in her chamber where the fire had died and the room could not possibly be warmer than the sub-zero temperatures outdoors, she collapsed on the settle, every appendage to her body trembling.

Miss Willets would never have stepped foot out of doors in this wretchedly wintry climate without her cherished furry boots.

With a painful acquiescence, Mary feared her old companion had been murdered—likely by the same person who tried to murder her last night. It saddened her horribly. And for the hundredth time, she wondered why anyone would ever wish to harm a harmless old lady.

As surely as she knew Stephen was all that was noble in word and deed, she knew evil lurked at Le Chateau.

Stephen had told her he would allow ten minutes for her to get in and out of the Italians' chamber, then he would meet her in his chamber. Woefully, neither of them had thought about her lack of a key to his room.

But Stephen was too intelligent not to realize, when he did come upstairs, that she would have had to take refuge in her own chamber, as frigid as it was. If he didn't hurry up, she might very well turn into an icicle.

Five minutes stretched to ten before she heard a man's heavy footfall followed by a tapping at her door. She went to it. "Pray, who's there?" She was still terrified the murderer would be angling for another chance to kill her.

"Stephen."

She opened the door and eyed him with mock disdain.

"Forgive me," he said. "I forgot to give you my key."

"I am well aware of that fact, my lord." She withdrew her lock and was only too happy to close the door behind her and go to his chamber, which was still invitingly warm. She went straight to the settle and made herself comfortable.

Standing, he looked down at her. "Well?"

She met his gaze somberly. "I am certain the boots belonged

to dear, sweet Miss Willets." Then in a fragile voice, she asked, "What do you think can have happened to her?"

"I wish I had an answer."

She patted the smoothly worn wooden settle seat beside her, and he came to sit there.

"Do you think it's possible she's still alive?" Mary asked.

"I wouldn't wager on it, but there could be a slim possibility she's alive, but where, I couldn't say."

"It's for certain she's not in the Italians' chamber. How do you suppose that woman got Miss Willets' boots? I'm quite sure they wouldn't even fit her. That Italian woman's almost as tall as her husband."

Stephen cleared his throat. "I don't think the Italians are married. To each other, at least."

"That explains it! I thought they were too smoochie koochie for long-married people."

"You witnessed them kissing?" he asked, his brows raised.

She shrugged. "Not actually, but it's just their general, overly affectionate manner. Married couples in their forties do not act like that, as a rule. What makes you think they're not married?"

"Not any one thing, just a few impressions. I believe the reason they pretend not to speak French or English is that they don't want to become acquainted with anyone here, except for Becker, who I believe hosts them twice a year for their little illicit affair. I have also noticed a disparity in their dress. I would say, judging from his clothing, the man—who refused to give me his name . . ."

"That's awfully telling, is it not?"

He nodded and continued. "The man appears to be wealthy, but I believe the Italian woman's clothes are not nearly as high a quality as her lover's, which tends to confirm she's not his wife. Mind you, I'm no arbiter of women's fashions, but I do have three clothing-mad sisters which has taught me a few things about women's tastes."

"How clever of you to notice that and how careless of me not to have. You may have noticed I'm rather a slave to fashion."

"Yes, I had."

"I must compliment you on your success in engaging them in conversation, but from the way I saw the woman smiling at you, I daresay she was taken with your handsomeness."

Stephen's mouth folded into a grim line, and he shook his head as if he'd just heard something with which he neither agreed nor approved. "I may have to start to believe like the others that you see things that don't exist."

"I gave you my vow I wouldn't lie to you."

He still looked annoyed.

"Do you suppose the Italians know we're lovers?" she asked.

"We're not lovers."

Now she gave him an annoyed glance, partly because she had come to wish they actually were lovers and partly because of his terse response. "Of course I know that. But do we not wish for the others to believe that we are?"

"We do, but you must know a real gentleman doesn't brag about such things."

She turned to eye him with keen appreciation. There was no doubt this was the man she had been waiting for since she left the schoolroom four years previously. She did not believe any of the men who had offered for her hand in marriage would ever have been as protective as this man against the sinister forces opposing her. She owed him so much and feared she would never be able to repay him. "I don't care what any of these odious people think of me."

"I agree none of them are worth your consideration, except in regards to your almost-successful murder or to their relationship to the governess, if she was a governess."

If she was a governess. How perceptive he was. It made sense that Miss Willets was not what she had portrayed herself to be. "I don't suppose Miss Willets actually was a governess."

"We used to have an . . . operative working in France as a governess in the home of a minister, and we gleaned much valuable information from her."

Mary spun toward him. "What did she look like?"

He shrugged. "I never saw her."

"Did you have knowledge of what age she might have been?"

He thwacked his forehead. "It never occurred to me there could possibly be any connection between our elderly spy and your Miss Willets, but now it does seem plausible. How stupid of me not to have realized it sooner."

As it was stupid of her not to have doubted the veracity of the lady's background. "Two heads, particularly the combination of mine and yours, I believe, are better than one. Do you not think we could make a formidable team?"

It seemed as if he were not listening to her at all. She could tell he was lost in thought, likely trying to remember everything he could about the Foreign Office's elderly female spy.

A considerable period of time passed before he finally spoke. "If your Miss Willets is our Miss Coney, she hasn't been authorized to advance to Vienna. She would only be doing so if she was in possession of vital information. We must make every effort to find her."

"That's what I've been trying to do for the past several days!"

"Well, my dear Lady Mary, we shall proceed." His brows quirked. "Do you hear that?"

CHAPTER FOURTEEN

M ARY LEAPT TO her feet and went to the window, pushing aside the homespun curtains as Stephen came to stand at her side. The outside cold penetrated the glass, causing her to hug herself for warmth. "That's one of my chair men shoveling snow on the left." She continued to watch the men toil beneath pewter skies and softly falling snow.

"My two are behind him, and Blanchard's chair man is working beside yours. They face a daunting prospect, considering the snow continues to fall."

"It was frightfully wretched last night—though, of course, Lord Stephen the Lusty Sleeper would not be privy to such information," she teased, eyeing him playfully, a look he returned. "I daresay the snow's more than a foot taller today than it was yesterday. Even if those fellows manage to clear a path, the new snow will just cover it up again."

"I don't know." A contemplative look settled on his face as he watched the workers. "The snow does seem to be falling at a much lighter rate."

"Perhaps. Do you think they're eager to get here because they have no food?"

"I doubt it. Becker told me they've stores of cheeses, wine, and roots here and in those outbuildings."

"I'm beastly disappointed not to see Miss Willets' chair men."

"Me, too. I would generously grease some palms to know what's become of them."

"And her."

"There is that."

She turned to smile at him. It occurred to her she'd become closer to him than she'd ever been to another man—not just because they were physically close as they were now or because she had slept, quite innocently, in the same bed with this man.

But in a very short time, she had come to know him well enough to anticipate when he was going to say *there is that*. She knew he was devoted to his sisters, and she had learned little things about him, like the fact he eschewed the glamorous trappings of London life in favor of his family's country estate.

She understood that he was governed by loyalty, loyalty to his crown and country as well as loyalty to her, a beleaguered woman he'd known for only a few days.

Looking into his pensive face brought her joy, especially when he returned her gaze as he was doing now. There was such strength in his face, and there was a spark of some indefinable emotion in his currant-black eyes as they held hers. Her heartbeat accelerated.

She felt his heat and, at first, thought she heard his heartbeat but realized it was her own drumming nearly out of her chest.

Unconscious of what she was doing, she moved even closer, her face still lifted to his.

His head lowered and his lips gently pressed hers.

The kiss deepened. Some indefinable onslaught of exhilaration spread through her body like liquid warmth as her arms came fully around him. She'd only been kissed like this once before, and that young man was long dead and finally a distant shadow to Stephen, dear beloved Stephen. She savored every moment of the kiss' drugging sensation.

When he crushed her into his embrace, she shuddered. She wasn't certain, but she thought he did, too.

Then as abruptly as the kiss had begun, he straightened,

breaking the embrace but keeping two strong hands on her shoulders. "Forgive me. I am not behaving as a gentleman ought."

"And I'm not behaving as a lady," she whispered.

"You are a lady, to be sure." He backed away—several feet away from her—and when he spoke, his voice was no longer soft and tender. "It's just that we must be cognizant that this environment can be conducive to such displays of intimacy. As your protector, it's my responsibility to guard your innocence, too."

Your protector. The very words cocooned her. Her insides caved. Regrettably, she wasn't quite innocent. Would that single indiscretion when she was sixteen deprive of her of happiness for the rest of her days? Would a man be able to tell? Would she be obliged to confess her lapse to a future husband?

Obviously, this man had no desire to be that future husband. He hadn't even wanted to prolong the kiss. But she would vow he had enjoyed every breathless second of it as much as she had.

It was not the heat of the nearby fire that stung her cheeks. She felt as if she'd been dismissed as one would cast aside an unwanted demirep. How could she have gone from such euphoria to humiliation in the span of a few seconds?

Straightening her shoulders and holding her head high, she returned to her place on the settle, which was warm to the touch. "Do you have any suggestions for how to confront the Italians?" she asked, changing the subject to deflect her embarrassment.

"It's a delicate situation that will require a considered approach." He paced the chamber as he deliberated.

As much as she wanted him sitting on the settle beside her, she understood why he'd chosen not to, but the knowledge did not alleviate her pain. "I say prohibit the considerate. The time has come for plain speaking with these shameful reprobates. This place is full of vile people who don't deserve a *considered approach.*"

He whirled toward her. "So what are you suggesting?"

"I plan to ask the woman why Miss Willets' shoes are in her possession." Her announcement met with a wall of silence.

"I foresee two problems with that approach," he finally said. "First, there's the problem with language. You don't speak in her tongue. Even though you know and I know that they can speak French, they're not going to own the ability to do so."

"But you, my dear lord, do speak Italian."

His brow hiked and the corners of his mouth twitched as if he were having difficulty suppressing a smile. "Have I ever offered to be your interpreter?"

She pouted like a spoiled child. "You have kindly offered to be my protector. Does interacting with the lying, stealing, possibly murdering co-inhabitants of Le Chateau not come under your duties as my gallant ally?"

The control he was exercising to evoke a stern look softened. "Possibly." As strong as he was both in character and in physical attributes, he was guided by his unerring sense of morality.

"And what is your second perceived obstacle?"

"How can you possibly explain your knowledge that Miss Willets' boots are in her possession without admitting to your unlawful search of their chamber?"

"While I have vowed not to lie to you, I have no objections to lying to the liars."

He laughed. "And so you're going to say exactly what?"

"I might just tell them that I overheard the blonde girl with braids—the one who replenishes the firewood in our chambers—God knows she doesn't clean the rooms. The girl was admiring the furry boots in the Italian lady's chamber."

"Oh, so I'm the one who's supposed to be delivering this piece of fabrication to the Italian woman? You're asking *me* to lie?"

She shook her head. "Of course not! I'll be the liar. You're merely to be the translator."

Shaking his head, he began to chuckle. "Breaking into others' rooms, stealthily plotting, lying, the next thing you'll have me tying up the other guests in ropes."

"That's a delightful prospect!"

He gave a mock growl. "After dinner we'll confront the Italians."

BECAUSE THE ITALIANS were neither given to socializing nor to lingering about anywhere other than their bedchamber, Stephen watched them throughout their typical dinner of boiled meat, cheeses, bread, and foul-tasting wine. He wanted to be in a position to pop up and engage them in conversation, possibly in the inglenook, as soon as they indicated their intention of leaving the eating room.

Though he'd initially been opposed to so openly speaking with the Italian woman about her possession of Miss Willets' boots, he realized now that Mary's plan had merit. They had spent far too many days complacently accepting the deviousness of the other inhabitants of Le Chateau. It was time he openly confronted these unscrupulous people.

That wasn't to say he was looking forward to it. He had always hated confrontations of any kind. Perhaps that's why he'd chosen the life of a diplomat. He craved congeniality. Among people. Among nations.

Another matter that caused him considerable consternation was today's kiss. It was difficult to sit across the table from this lovely woman and not recall how profoundly that most tender yet sexually potent that kiss had affected him. How could such heated passions simmer below the surface of this young woman who resembled a perfect piece of Dresden porcelain?

He could not purge his mind of how incredibly desirable she was. It grew more and more difficult to think of her as Devere's little sister.

Even the memory of their kiss aroused him. Which wouldn't

do at all.

She was merely grateful to him for believing her, for caring about her welfare, for vowing to defend her against the disreputable lot of fellow guests—and their host.

When he observed the Italians scooting their chairs away from the table, he nodded to Mary, who immediately set down her fork, scooped up her napkin, and set it on the table beside her unfinished plate.

As the Italians passed their table, he nodded at them, smiling broadly, and he and Mary rose, following them. Upon clearing the chamber's door, he spoke to them in Italian. "Please, may I have a word?" His gaze shifted to the inglenook. "Perhaps we could sit here for a moment."

The man and woman glanced at Mary, exchanged puzzled looks, then nodded and sat on the bench opposite from where Stephen and Mary normally sat. He wasn't sure how he was going to proceed, but Mary took the reins by starting her conversation in English.

"The lady here, Lady Mary Beresford, has asked me to interpret for her because she does not speak Italian."

Brows lowered as they looked at her, both nodded.

Mary continued, and he translated. "Lady Mary says that she overheard the girl who brings the logs to our chamber remark about the fur boots in your chamber, and Lady Mary believes they may have belonged to her missing friend. She claims that the description of the boots sounds exactly like those belonging to her friend and that they're one of a kind made by a now-dead man in little French village."

The Italian woman's eyes rounded. "Would Lady Mary care to see the boots?" she asked.

He translated.

Mary favored the lady with a beaming smile. "I should love to."

The woman promptly left, raced up the stairs, and came back in a few moments, handing the boots to Mary.

"As you can probably tell," the Italian woman said to Stephen, "they are too small for me. Perhaps Lady Mary can wear them? No?"

Stephen translated.

Mary untied her left half boot and slipped her small stockinged foot into the proffered one being offered by the Italian woman. "Yes, they do fit me," Mary said solemnly. "How is it these came into your possession?" Mary removed it, replacing it with her own, and hugged the boots close to her breast as one would a pet cat or small dog.

Stephen translated.

Now the Italian woman faced Mary and spoke in her native tongue. "They were in our chamber when we arrived. I think the previous owner missed them when packing. The former occupant must have removed them upon getting into her bed, but they got partially under the bed and must have been overlooked. I thought they were beautiful, that they might fit my daughter, but it does not actually get that cold where we reside."

My daughter, not *our daughter*. A telling word that could possibly confirm they were not married to each other. Nodding, Stephen said, "That's right. You live in the sunny south." He had thought it odd anyone would choose to holiday in the frigid mountains when they could be enjoying the mild Mediterranean climate.

He informed Mary of the woman's last comment.

"Ask her what she was told of their room's last guest," Mary said.

He repeated.

The woman looked at the man. Both shook their heads. "We were told nothing."

"Ask if they ever saw a silver-haired lady with spectacles."

He did.

Again, the woman and man looked at each other, but it was the man who answered. "We never saw an old silver-haired lady."

Stephen translated.

Mary's shoulders slumped. She turned sorrowful eyes on the couple and thanked them.

CHAPTER FIFTEEN

S TEPHEN WENT TO his valet's chamber in order to give Mary privacy to dress for bed and to explain to Humphrey why his services would be greatly reduced until the weather cleared and the journey continued.

Mary's presence in Stephen's chamber had all but stripped the valet of his duties. It wouldn't have done at all to have the man in the same chamber with a maiden. Poor Humphrey. He lamented that he was nothing more than a charity case who was not being permitted to earn his keep. The man's subdued yet dramatic sense of persecution was comical.

Sometimes when dealing with his valet, Stephen felt like a puppet master expertly controlling the strings, balancing praise with requests in a delicate give-and-take. "You are the best valet any man has ever had," Stephen assured. "And once we're on our way to Vienna, you will return to your normal routine—a prospect of which I am only too eager to resume." In more ways than in being expertly dressed.

After smoothing Humphrey's ruffled feathers, Stephen returned to his chamber. The candles had been extinguished and only the light from the glowing fireplace illuminated the room.

It was a moment before he saw her. She sat on the settle facing the fire. Unlike the previous night, this night she wore a snow white, soft linen night shift that exposed much of her silken flesh—and caused him to sharply draw in his breath.

She slowly turned to face him, firelight captured in her silvery gold locks, a questioning look on her lovely face.

"I wish you wouldn't do this to me," he growled.

"Do what?" she asked in an unquestioningly innocent voice.

He was powerless to remove his gaze from her, powerless to keep from lazily perusing the beautiful woman from the tip of her shimmering hair to the delectable swell of her breasts to the dainty feet she was attempting to tuck beneath her. "Making me regret my vow to remain a gentleman."

Her beautifully arched brows lowered. "But you are a gentleman."

What an innocent! Did she not understand her own seductive powers? He drew a deep breath. "I am a man, and when you dress like that you make me regret that I've vowed to be a gentleman."

Their gazes locked, then her lashes lowered. A somber silence filled the chamber like the stoppage of a heartbeat.

A moment passed before she looked up at him. "Given what you've just said, I don't suppose you'll want to sit beside me."

"That's correct." He continued to stand, his gaze boring down on her.

"I should like to ask you a question."

"I am at your service, my lady." He strove for formality, grasping for something to dispel this intoxicating effect she had upon him.

Now she drew in a breath. "I'm asking for my friend, and I'm asking you because I believe you're of noble character and make sound judgments."

What the devil? He shrugged. "I don't know about that, but I appreciate your compliment. What is it you want to ask?"

"My friend . . . who is the same age as me committed an indiscretion when she was sixteen."

His brow arched. "An indiscretion?"

She nodded. "With the brother of her best friend. He was five years older than she and knew quite a bit more of the world than . . . my friend, who fancied herself in love with him. He was leaving the following day for the Peninsula and told her he might be slain on a foreign battlefield." Her voice dropped to a somber tone. "Which later proved to be an accurate premonition."

"It would be difficult to grieve a man who preyed on a young girl's affection in such a manner."

"I believe he did take advantage of her. The . . . indiscretion was not what she wanted." Mary paused, her voice breaking.

His thoughts went to his sister, Sarah. Stephen would have considered killing any so-called friend of his who stole his sister's innocence, especially at the tender age of sixteen.

Why was Mary bringing this up with him? What was she going to ask?

"My friend doesn't know if she's obliged to reveal this dark secret to a future husband. What do you think she should do?"

It suddenly became clear to him she wasn't asking for her friend. Mary herself must have been taken advantage of when she was sixteen. A cacophony of emotions slammed into him. Anger at the blighter. Compassion for the girl she'd been. But most of all, tenderness for this young woman who'd been made to feel damaged by the actions of a selfish man.

It was a moment before he could respond. "I cannot guide your friend. I believe she should be free to enter a marriage as would one who is pure and who deserves a loving union with a man who will cherish her."

Tears began to trickle from Mary's eyes.

He rushed to sit next to her and draw her into his arms. Her softness, her petite size, her light rose scent were all very much to his liking. She began to sob, and it tore at his heart.

"It doesn't matter, Mary, my dearest. The man you eventually bestow your love upon will be a most fortunate man."

She whimpered. "It's you, Stephen. And I've felt beastly that you considered me an innocent when I'm not."

It's you? God in heaven, did that mean she thought she had fallen in love with him? He separated just enough to kiss her forehead. "But you *are* an innocent. You can't be blamed for the depravity of what I can only refer to as an evil man. Dead or not." He kissed her forehead once more. "I'm flattered by your regard, but you merely mistake your gratitude to me for love."

Possessing her love now seemed something to be desired.

She shook her head. "I've come to love everything about you," she murmured. "I've never felt that way about any man before."

Is that why she'd dressed in such a revealing manner tonight? Was she offering herself to him?

He felt as if his chest had expanded by six inches. The control he'd always prided himself on suddenly dissolved. His heartbeat roared. The blood pumped fast and hot through his veins and settled in his groin as he crushed her to him for a hungry kiss. Her lips willingly parted beneath the bruising pressure of his mouth.

She fitted to him as if she'd been created expressly for such a purpose. He was consumed by this woman, by everything about her from her loveliness to the feel of her soft flesh to the very taste of her, but she offered so much more than the physical. This woman was offering him her heart.

His own heart was exploding with these new, overwhelming emotions. Mary loved him—Mary who would risk everything for those she loved. She'd shown it with Miss Willets.

And now she was showing him that he meant more to her than protecting her good name. She was offering herself, the ultimate offering.

But could he allow himself to accept? He'd never wanted anything more.

Her shift slipped from an ivory shoulder and her full breast sprang loose. He groaned, his breathing accelerating as if he'd just run uphill. Still, he told himself he should resist. Then their gazes met. She made no effort to act coy or to conceal the sultry desire that flamed in her eyes.

She had taken the decision out of his hands.

He kissed a trail of feathery kisses along the curve of her lovely neck and farther still until he drew a perfect pink nipple into his mouth. She whimpered, tightening her hold on him, and he thought he could go mad with the intensity of his desire.

As some men craved their opium, he craved this union with this woman. This woman and no other. Groaning with want, he scooped her into his arms and carried her to the bed.

Her eyelids heavy with need, she lay there and watched in the dim light as he stripped bare and came to lie beside her. When she curled against him, he was nearly overcome with powerful feelings unlike anything he'd ever experienced. He wanted her. Everything about her. He wanted to stroke her silken flesh, to feel her tongue mingle with his, to blend with this woman who'd bestowed her love on him.

But he wanted even more. He wanted—no, needed—to spend the rest of his life ensuring that he was worthy of her love. He wanted to protect her for as long as they should live. He wanted to always be the one to chuckle at her breezily delivered exaggerations. He wanted her face to be the first thing he saw each morning. He wanted this woman to bear his children. He wanted her now and for the rest of his days.

With hands as well as mouth, he touched her everywhere, until she begged for release. Only then did he part her thighs and sink into her with his velvety length, gently at first then at her urging, faster and harder, surging and retreating. Two bodies trembled, stilled, shuddered. Two voices cried out in pleasure.

Slick with their own heat, they lay in the peace of each other for a long time afterward. He could not imagine ever parting from Mary, his Mary. It was as if she'd etched herself onto his soul.

SHE'D NEVER FELT happier, never felt so loved, never felt so complete. Stephen may not have told her he loved her, but she knew he did. He'd been a gentle lover, one more concerned with giving her pleasure than in taking his own. Even before that ultimate act, even though she knew he had to be throbbing with need, he would not proceed until she hungrily encouraged him.

When she awakened to murky dawn, it was as if her whole body smiled while, her eyes softly closed, she lay in the warmth of the bed—their bed, she thought, flush with his possession. What complete joy she had known throughout the night in this bed with the most desirable man ever created. Heat from a fresh fire filled the chamber. Stephen would be responsible for that, she thought with glowing pride.

Clutching the eiderdown to her chest, she eased up to a seated position, casting her gaze toward the fire. She'd expected he'd be near the fire or settle, but he wasn't. Disappointed, she decided to dress before he returned to the chamber. She left the bed and donned her pale blue velvet gown. A pity her lover wasn't there to help lace her into her stays. All previous sense of embarrassment over displaying her bare body had fled after last night's lovemaking.

Every cell in her body screamed of his possession. She belonged to Stephen.

When she finished dressing, he still hadn't returned. She would like to sit in front of the fire and read, but she'd finished all her books. Would Stephen have something she could read? She went to the bedside table and opened the drawer. What she saw there caused her heart to race nearly out of her chest. Fury gripped her.

There in his drawer was a miniature portrait of her. How had it come into Stephen's possession? This meeting at Le Chateau was no chance encounter. Was he in league with those responsible for Miss Willets' disappearance?

CHAPTER SIXTEEN

SINCE MARY SHOWED no inclination to awaken, Stephen decided to pop down to the end of the corridor and climb the narrow staircase there to the garret where the guests' servants' rooms were located. This early morning would be a good time to tidy up his own appearance and to repair Humphrey's bruised pride.

He had no doubts his valet would be awake even though it was only barely past dawn. He was right. A perfectly dressed Humphrey immediately responded to Stephen's knock on his chamber door. "My lord?" A shocked expression marked the man's fleshy face as his dark brows hiked.

Stephen held out his crumpled cravat. "Be a good man and do your magic on this for me."

Though Humphrey was not given to overt displays of emotion, a hint of a smile tweaked at his lips. "Should you care to come in while I iron this for your lordship?"

Though Humphrey had served him half his life, Stephen had never before entered his servant's private chambers. "Thank you for offering," Stephen said as he stepped into the room.

The chamber was exactly what Stephen would have expected to find. The bed coverings had been tidily restored, all table surfaces were free of clutter, and the man's meager wardrobe hung neatly in his slender portmanteau—the total opposite of

Mary.

Stephen chuckled to himself over Mary's tendencies to haphazardly strew whatever chamber she was in with clothing, books, and toiletry items. Even a passing thought of her caused his heartbeat to flicker and infused him with a deep sense of possessiveness. Her untidiness could be overlooked. She had far more desirable attributes. Making love with her had been the single most profound experience of his entire thirty years.

"I shall have to improvise with the iron, my lord, but I have every confidence things will come out to your satisfaction."

Stephen watched with fascination as his man used tongs to remove pieces of hot metal from the fireplace and put them in the iron's hinged opening.

"I use coals at home—and, of course, have a special implement that fits next to the fire to keep the iron hot, but there's only so much one can bring on a long journey like this," Humphrey explained.

"Indeed. Much has to be sacrificed, but you've done a splendid job."

After the valet ironed the fine linen cravat, he expertly tied it around his employer's neck. "If your lordship would care to bring me your extra cravats I can wash and iron them for another day's use."

Never before had Humphrey suggested Stephen come to his chamber. Such an invitation was testament to the valet's consideration of Mary. "Very good of you. I shall do that." Stephen was only too happy to return to the woman with whom he'd fallen in love, but as he entered the corridor he was dismayed to see her lugging her portmanteau behind her, returning to her old chamber.

Good lord! Had his lovemaking been that disappointing? Last night, she'd certainly seemed to enjoy every intoxicating moment in his arms. "Pray, my lady, what do you think you're doing?" He effected a stern voice as he approached her. She wore the dress he most admired on her, one the same soft shade of blue as her spectacular eyes. The sight of her stirred his lust.

She ignored him and stormed toward her chamber.

Stunned by her rejection yet too much in love to take it stoically, he came abreast of her and set a hand to her arm. "What's happened?"

She brushed his hand away and rounded on him. Her eyes blazed with searing anger, and when she spoke, her voice was harsh. "You're a fraud."

He felt as if he'd been slapped in the face.

Her pocket yielded the key to the lock, which easily opened, and she moved into the chamber.

He stuck his foot in the door's opening so she wouldn't shut him out. Then he stepped in, yanked the heavy portmanteau away from her, and placed it near the window. There was no temperature difference between this frigid chamber and the outdoors. "I deserve an explanation."

She reached into her pocket and withdrew something small. Then she turned the miniature—the one he'd been given by her brother—to face him.

His insides dropped. His eyelids lowered. He cursed under his breath. "I beg that you allow me to explain."

"There's nothing you can say to erase the fact you've been grossly dishonest."

"Never dishonest. I did omit telling the complete truth."

"Whatever you've been to me has been a lie. I thought you were a gallant, rescuing knight. I imbued you with every noble quality a man could possibly possess." Her eyes misted. Her voice broke. "Twice now, I've been ruined by unworthy men."

He moved to her, setting a gentle hand on her arm. "You're right about me being unworthy but totally wrong about being ruined. What occurred between us last night was beautiful. Two consenting adults professed to love one another. I have never been more sincere in my affections."

She shook her head. "You can no longer claim my trust. For all I know, you're involved in Miss Willets' disappearance."

"You can't possibly believe that! You have to trust me. I'm the only one here who has your best interest at heart."

Rubbing her arms for warmth, she strode past him as if he did not exist. "I'm going to ask them to come start a fire in my chamber. It's chilly in here."

AFTER REQUESTING THE girl with braids see to it that a fire was started in her corner chamber, Mary strode across the eating room to the back wall, smiling and nodding to the Italians as she passed them. She took a table near them—and far away from where she customarily sat with Stephen.

The despair she'd felt when she was used and abandoned at sixteen couldn't touch what she felt today. Then, she'd had living parents who cherished her. She had siblings who would, as later proved to be the case, sacrifice their own happiness for her. She'd had a devoted maid, many good friends, and beautiful places to live. And she was safe from harm.

Now, she was completely alone. Someone under this roof wanted her dead. Everyone here lied. Especially Stephen. She could trust no one.

One day's difference between dark and daylight was stark. Last night, she'd been blissfully happy in Stephen's arms. As long as she had him, she'd been convinced nothing bad could ever happen to her, none of the evil surrounding them mattered, she had so blindly thought.

He had shielded her like the walls of a mighty castle. Now, the castle was in ruins.

Even more melancholy weighted her at the memory of the words he'd spoken just moments before. *I've never been more sincere in my affections.* It was a backhanded declaration of his love, but how could she ever believe him again?

It terrified her that she might never reach Vienna. She could very well die here in these forlorn and freezing mountains. Her family might never learn her wretched fate.

The more she thought about dying here on this frozen piece of earth, the more dread filled her like a sea fog penetrating every pore in her body. She'd been in want of a brain to have set off on so perilous a journey by herself. She had only her foolish self to blame for the woes that now befell her and her bleak—though likely shortened—future.

Yesterday, with Stephen at her side, she'd felt invincible. Her confidence in him was so great, she had believed he would make everything right. He would find Miss Willets alive. He would single-handedly dispatch those responsible for her disappearance and for the attempt on Mary's life. She and he would set off for Vienna, carefree and secure in their love for one another.

Today, she had no hope.

When she saw the form of a tall man standing in the doorway of the eating room, she knew it was him. She looked up from her steaming cup of tea just enough to confirm the man was Stephen but not enough to make eye contact with the brooding man staring at her.

Undeterred by her stiffness, he strode across the chamber to her table. When he went to pull out a chair, she stopped him. "You're not wanted here."

The dejected look on his face would have troubled her previously, but now she was unmoved. His deception outweighed any former good qualities the man may have possessed.

"I have to talk to you," he said.

"Have I not already made it clear I don't wish to speak to you?"

"Have I not shown you I'm the only one here who cares about you? Can you not believe how deeply I care for you?"

Her heartbeat thumped. She still had refused to look him in the eyes. *He cares for me deeply.* She had believed that last night. Now she didn't know what to believe. All she understood was this festering hurt that had been inflicted upon her by his deception.

She finally directed a cold glare at him. "I've asked you to leave my table. If you don't, I shall be forced to forgo my breakfast and return to *my* chamber."

"I don't like you being in that chamber."

"But it matters not to me what you like." She yanked her gaze away from him and stirred more sugar into her tea.

He continued standing in front of her. She continued ignoring him.

Before he left, he spoke authoritatively. "If you, headstrong woman that you are, persist in returning to your previous chamber, I insist that you use my locks. They cannot be compromised. And I'm better equipped than you to defend myself." He stalked away to their former table.

STEPHEN KNEW SHE would not respond if he were to knock on her door. Desperate to speak with her, he spent the day reading in the inglenook, hoping she would come there. He had to explain everything. In hindsight, he realized he should have told her the complete truth as soon as the relationship between them began to veer toward intimacy.

When light from the nearby window waned, he realized it would soon be dinnertime. She wasn't going to come. He started to return to his chamber to dress for dinner.

He might as well let Humphrey do the honors. He would just pop up to his valet's room to request his services. He climbed the narrow staircase to the garret and knocked upon the man's door, surprised that there wasn't an immediate answer. It wasn't as if Humphrey played cards. The man had no vices, only virtues.

Perhaps he'd gone to sleep. Stephen knocked loudly, and this time followed the knock by calling out the man's name. Still, there was no response.

It was then that Stephen realized a noticeable chill emanating from his valet's chamber. This wasn't like Humphrey at all. Though the fellow revealed very little personal information about himself, he'd been unable to conceal from his employer his intense dislike of the cold.

Why the devil was Humphrey's chamber so beastly cold? For reasons he was incapable of understanding, Stephen was certain something was amiss. Brows lowered, he yanked on the door handle, put his weight against the door, and heaved it open.

There was no sign of Humphrey. Which, he supposed, was good, given Stephen's worry. But, oddly, the window was opened fully.

Stephen crossed the chamber and peered out. Though it was nearly dark now, Stephen's worries were confirmed. There was no mistake. Sprawled on the mounds of snow was his valet's lifeless body.

CHAPTER SEVENTEEN

S TEPHEN PRACTICALLY FLEW down three flights of stairs. A winded Becker greeted him when he reached the ground floor. The innkeeper's face collapsed with concern. "Is something the matter, my lord? You're running like the house is on fire." His gaze raked over Stephen. "And you look a fright."

"We must go outside. I fear my valet's been killed."

"Killed? How?"

Stephen hurried to the outer door. "He plunged from his garret room."

"Then . . . his body is outside?"

Stephen nodded grimly.

Becker set a gentle hand on Stephen's forearm. "You can't go out with no coat. Wait a moment and I'll fetch my old coat for you." He patted his round belly. "I have outgrown it."

A minute later, he returned wearing gloves and a long woolen great coat and carrying a similar one for Stephen.

Outdoors, they sank into snow that, were it not so tightly packed, would have buried them. They plodded along until they intersected the path the chair men had been working on all day. The workers had never reached the earth's surface but had managed to scoop out a path some three feet beneath the snow's ever-mounting surface.

Stephen and Becker followed this up to the chalet's corner,

where they turned northward to Humphrey's body, which lay half a dozen feet away.

With every step that sank into fresh snow, Stephen prayed his faithful retainer would still be alive, though every ounce of reason he possessed told him that was not going to be the case. Humphrey had fallen a full four stories. Such an impact would be bound to have crushed his skull.

And even if he survived the fall, he would probably have succumbed to the elements. The temperatures were below zero.

When he came upon the body, Stephen winced in horror. Humphrey had fallen face first. It would be a miracle if the impact had not broken his neck. Humphrey's black-clad body sprawled on the ice, snow beginning to cover him. Snow mounded upon the man's bare hands. There was no doubt he was dead. He'd been there for at least an hour.

Becker came up just behind Stephen. He looked first at the body, then turned to Stephen, whose grief had caused tears to pool. Without saying a word, Becker bent down to feel for a pulse. Seconds later, he straightened and shook his head solemnly. "Give me a hand. We'll put him into the ice house."

As they lugged Humphrey's body the twenty feet to the ice house, a deep sense of loss crushed Stephen. What a fine man Humphrey had been. No one ever had a more loyal servant. The man's greatest pride came when Stephen was impeccably turned out. Humphrey had once confessed that he kept all the newspaper accounts that mentioned his master.

Humphrey would be gravely missed. And he could never be replaced.

Under normal circumstances, Stephen's chilled, ungloved hands in these sub-freezing temperatures would be a source of pain. But not now, not when there was a much greater source of pain, the kind of pain that would not respond to physical ministrations.

"Poor sod must have decided to do himself in," Becker said.

Stephen glared at the older man. "Humphrey would never do

such a thing. I've known him half my life."

Becker stopped in front of the door to the ice house and opened it. It was as dark as the interior of a cave.

Was this the last time Stephen would ever see Humphrey? Such a painful thought. As difficult as it was, he knelt beside the body and peered into his valet's unseeing black eyes. Drawing in a fortifying breath, he lowered Humphrey's eyelids. It was then he noticed something odd. Something horrifying. A piece of cloth had been stuffed into Humphrey's mouth. "Someone wanted to ensure none of us heard his screams as my good man fell to his death."

Becker's sullen gaze locked with Stephen's. "Surely you're not suggesting this is murder?"

"That's exactly what I'm suggesting."

STEPHEN HOPED HE could catch the servants who billeted in the garret before they left to prepare their masters for dinner. He was in luck, if one could find anything lucky on so grim a day. The Italians' servant, whose room was next to Humphrey's, was in his chamber.

The young man did not invite Stephen into his narrow room, nor did he fully open the door. Stephen queried him in his native tongue. Had he seen anyone come to the next room belonging to the Englishman?

The curly-haired Italian shook his head.

"You've been here all day?"

The other man shrugged. "Except when I had permission to use the washroom. I needed to launder my master's cravats."

"And when would that have been?"

The other man puckered his lips in thought. "Between two and three this afternoon."

That fit with Stephen's estimate of the time of death. He

drilled the other fellow suspiciously. "Did anyone see you in the laundry room?"

The Italian shrugged. "The one with the large bosom and blonde braids saw me coming and going, as I had to walk past her."

Stephen thanked him and moved to the chamber on the other side of Humphrey's room. Blanchard's man answered, smiling at Stephen. *"Bonjour."* The five of them—Stephen and two Belgians along with Stephen's and Blanchard's capable valets—had been traveling together for nearly two weeks now. Humphrey had appeared to get along well with the Belgians though they could not speak in the other's language.

"I'm afraid I have some bad news," Stephen said in French.

The Belgian's brows squeezed together.

"My . . ." Stephen's voice began to splinter. "My valet has been killed."

A look of terror crossed the man's face. "How?"

"I believe one or more persons came to his chamber." Stephen drew a breath. "He was pushed from his open window."

An agonized expression on his face, the valet tightly shut his eyes and softly cursed. It took a moment for him to gather his wits.

"Would we not have heard him scream?"

"Cloth had been stuffed into his mouth. That is one of the reasons I believe two men must have done it."

"Yes. Monsieur Humphrey was a large man. It wouldn't have been easy to subdue him."

"Did you see anyone come to his chamber today?"

The servant shook his head, fear searing his mossy eyes.

"Then I don't suppose you heard anything either?"

"Nothing. But I was away from my chamber much of the afternoon."

"Do you mind telling me where you went?"

"Not at all, my lord. The Frenchmen who arrived here before us paid me to launder their shirts and cravats as they travel without valets."

Stephen found that surprising, given that the Frenchmen, unlike most of their countrymen, did not appear to be concerned in the least about their shabby appearance.

The Belgian shook his head forlornly. "Why would anyone want to kill Monsieur Humphrey?"

"I have no answer for that."

"This place is sinister. I've felt it for days."

"Indeed it is."

In his bedchamber, Stephen paced the floor. Why would anyone want to kill Humphrey? The tender-hearted, exceedingly congenial fellow couldn't possibly have an enemy in the world. The only plausible explanation—not that it explained anything—was that Humphrey's death was tied to Miss Willets' disappearance. And to the attempted murder of Mary. But how could Humphrey have been involved?

Stephen might never learn the details, but the evildoers must have thought Humphrey knew something about their vile schemes. Had he overheard something which endangered his life? Or had he perhaps seen something?

One thing Stephen knew for certain. Evil lurked at this inn.

Though he had no appetite, Stephen attempted to make himself presentable enough to go to the eating room. All the guests had preceded him, including Mary, who still sat against the back wall and avoided looking at him.

Whether she wanted to communicate with him or not, he strode to her table.

She looked up but offered no greeting.

"My valet's been murdered."

Her eyes widened. "Oh, Stephen, I'm so sorry." She indicated for him to sit.

He took a seat in the chair opposite her.

"What happened?" she asked.

"He was pushed from his garret window this afternoon."

"How tragic. You are sure it wasn't suicide?"

"I'm sure."

"Why did we not hear anything?"

"Cloth had been shoved into his mouth."

She winced. "Then there must have been at least two killers."

"My thoughts exactly."

Even though she'd never met Humphrey, her eyes filled with tears. "This is such an evil place, and I fear it's the last place I'll ever see."

He covered her hand, but she pulled it away.

"I wasn't lying," he said, "when I told you I would never allow harm to come to you."

"Even a large man like you would be handicapped against two or more men—men who I'm beginning to believe have been trained to kill."

Like her, he had come to believe assassins had been put on the trail of Miss Willets, and the more he thought on it, the more convinced he became that Miss Willets was really Miss Coney. "As unworthy as I am, I offer myself as your knight protector."

The corners of her mouth turned down. "You remembered."

"I remember everything about you." *Especially last night.* Every move, every murmured word, every caress. "You must permit me to protect you."

She stiffened. "No. I no longer trust you. For all I know, you're in league with *them.*"

"You can't possibly believe that. You know me better."

"I thought I did. I was mistaken."

"I'll explain. I was sent by Devere."

Her brows hiked. "You omitted to tell me you are acquainted with my brother." All semblance of congeniality was gone from her voice.

"I really don't know him that well. We were at Oxford at the same time, though he was two years ahead of me."

"Which college?" she quizzed, her gaze harsh.

Did she think he was lying about knowing Devere? "Christ Church."

Her face softened almost imperceptivity as she nodded. "Are you saying you barely know my brother?"

"While we are not well acquainted, I've always had profound respect for him. You will agree that Devere is universally well liked?"

She sighed. "I am convinced you *do* know my brother. Tell me, though, if you're not close friends, why did he . . . oh, I see. He knew you were coming to the Congress of Vienna."

"Yes. He graciously offered to pay me to look out for your welfare but, of course, I couldn't accept money for doing what any gentleman ought to do. I know if it were my sister, Devere would have obliged me."

"Indeed, he would have. Taking care of others has always been my brother's highest priority. And, I will add, he's the finest man I've ever known."

"I agree."

"So he gave you my miniature?"

He nodded.

"You should have told me the truth."

"Forgive me. If you will but trust me, I vow I will never again conceal anything from you."

She folded her arms in front of her and watched him, her eyes inscrutable. "I will trust you, but I'm a different woman today than I was yesterday. Those feelings I had for you then are gone."

As much as her words hurt, he knew he deserved them. She no longer wished to make love with him. He could not dwell on his own disappointment. All that mattered now was that he keep her alive. "You will stay in my chamber tonight."

She nodded solemnly. "But I will not be the fool I was last night."

CHAPTER EIGHTEEN

"I'LL HELP YOU move back to my chamber," Stephen said.

Her face saddened. "Poor Humphrey. It was so good of him to move my things the last time."

"He was a good man."

"You'd had him for long?"

"Since my days at Oxford."

"I suppose it's rather like losing a member of your family." Mary couldn't help feeling she was partially responsible for his death. Had she placidly accepted Miss Willets' disappearance and continued on with the journey, none of these other evil things would have occurred.

"Yes."

"On a brighter note, I shan't be too embarrassed for you to see my untidiness this time."

He flashed a white-toothed smile. Why did every facet of the man's appearance have to be so perfect? It made it even more difficult to deny him. "Because you haven't had enough time to be your messy self?" he asked playfully.

"Oh, it doesn't take me long to make mammoth messes, but the reason I won't be humiliated is because I plan to tidy things up myself before permitting you to see my chamber."

One by one, their fellow diners finished eating and left the room until she and Stephen were the only ones left.

"You say *tidy things up myself* as if it's an uncommon occurrence. Have you been that pampered throughout your life?"

"Indeed I have. And aren't you as guilty as I? Going off to Oxford with your own valet?"

"I suppose I am guilty. But, I daresay, I am by nature a tidy person."

Of course Lord Perfect was tidy by nature! And when he selected a bride she, too, would be perfect. A far cry from Mary. Which made her unhappy even though she was determined not to capitulate to her own ravishing desire for him.

She had humiliated herself all too often. What a massive fool she'd been to mistake his interest in her welfare for something stronger, more romantic. She didn't know if she should be angry with Devere or not. Were it not for her brother, she would never have known Stephen, never have fallen in love with him, never have been so colossally hurt.

"I'll just pop up to my room and put all my things neatly into my valise and portmanteau for you to collect," she said.

"While you're doing that, I need to speak with Becker about . . . what we're going to do with Humphrey."

She winced.

They left the eating room and parted a few feet from Becker's door.

Though it was early night with much life left, the staircase was eerily dark and quiet. A few wall sconces lighted the first floor she came to, but as she climbed to her floor, she realized the sconces there had not yet been lit.

The corridor was so dark that she couldn't even read the numbers on the doors. Her first inclination was to go back to Stephen. But how silly would that look at barely six in the evening? Nobody would be bold enough to accost her when everyone at the inn was still awake. And surely they or he or whoever it was wouldn't wish to commit two murders in the same day.

At the thought of poor Humphrey's death, a chill spiked up

her spine. Once more, dread filled her like stain upon a rug.

Since her chamber was the last one, it didn't matter that she could not read the room numbers. As she neared her door, a floorboard creaked just feet away. Terror bolted through her. She shook uncontrollably. He mustn't know that she knew the murderer awaited her. If he had a knife, her life could be instantly snuffed. She must try to stay calm as she stealthily retreated. As soundlessly as possible, she pivoted and retraced her steps back to the stairs as quietly as she could. When she was close to the staircase, her speed increased and she all but hurled herself down the stairs, her heartbeat exploding.

She was too terrified to turn back but kept hurrying down the two flights of stairs until she reached the ground floor. And Stephen.

He had been speaking with Becker until she intruded. He whirled at her, a questioning look on his face until he got a good look at her. "What's wrong?"

"Quick! He's up there!" Oddly, now that she was no longer clomping down the wooden treads, she heard no sign of anyone else descending the staircase.

Stephen started for the stairs, with Becker on his heels. "Who?"

"The murderer."

She wasn't about to stay alone downstairs or anywhere else. She followed them as they raced upstairs.

When they reached the landing of her floor, Becker cursed. "Why has that girl of mine not lighted these sconces?"

"I'll get a candle in my chamber," Stephen said.

Mary was dismayed that they'd not passed anyone. Stephen soon returned with a lighted candle and quickly determined that no one lurked in this dark corridor. The culprit had vanished just as Miss Willets had. Stephen gave her a sympathetic shrug, then turned to Becker. "My valet's murder is, no doubt, putting the lady on edge. We would appreciate it if you'd see the corridor remains lighted—all night would be preferable."

"Yes, of course, my lord," Becker said.

After Becker started back down the stairs, Stephen moved to her and lowered his voice. "I'm not letting you out of my sight."

Without him saying the words, she knew he believed her accusations were warranted.

She nodded and opened her chamber door. It no longer mattered that he see evidence of her slovenliness. Such silly pride was inconsequential given the terror she'd so recently experienced.

Within minutes, the move from her chamber to his was complete. Once he set down her weighty portmanteau, he came to her and drew her into his arms. "I'm sorry I wasn't here for you. It won't happen again."

Even though she had vowed not to succumb to this desirable man, at this moment, after what she'd experienced, she needed to feel herself enveloped in the comfort of his arms. She gloried in the warmth of his embrace. Why was it when she was with him like this she never felt threatened? How could she have such complete confidence in him? He was only one man up against incalculably sinister forces.

She had no right to feel so secure when the cost of her security could be his life as well as hers. What had she done? She'd dragged him into danger from which they might never be extricated.

He led her to the settle, where they sat in front of the inviting fire. "Tell me what happened," he said in a low, reassuring voice.

"I never saw him."

"Of course you didn't. The corridor was in total darkness."

She told him what she had experienced.

"I'm very proud of you," he said. "It's possible he did possess a knife. Had you not acted so promptly and stealthily . . ." He paused, drew a breath, and shook his head. "I fear you wouldn't be sitting here right now."

"I'm not so certain now that I acted correctly."

"What do you mean?"

"I probably should have screamed out so others might have

come, and the murderer could have been revealed."

"As much as I would like to unmask the evil man—or men—it would not have been worth the risk of your life." He squeezed her hand.

Her erratic breathing betrayed her. Why was it his every touch unlocked something wildly exciting within her? "Oh, Stephen, I'm so frightened. First Miss Willets, then your valet, and I'm to be next."

"That is evidently his—or their—objective. Which means our course must change."

"How?"

"We've been too passive, too reluctant for a confrontation."

"True."

"The time for complacency is past. We must be the aggressors."

She shook her head. "No. I can't permit you to jeopardize your life. It's me they want dead."

"And I cannot permit you to jeopardize your life." His intense gaze met hers, and a smile tweaked at his mouth. "I could never face Devere."

She playfully swatted at him. "So what do you propose? It's not as if you're equipped to face murdering cutthroats, singular or plural."

"I plan to enlist Becker's help."

Her mouth gaped open. "You cannot be serious! He's in with them."

He nodded. "Yes, I believe he was. I also believe he would never have consented to help them had he known they were murderers. You should have seen how upset he was over Humphrey's death. I'm certain he had no knowledge that the person or persons he was aiding intended to commit murder."

"That does relieve me. I'd gotten to where I was terrified to be around Mr. Becker. Do you really think you can enlist him to help us?"

"Indeed I do."

HE WASN'T ABOUT to leave Mary alone. With each of them armed with their knives, the two of them left his room. He locked the door and looked in both directions of the corridor. The girl with blonde braids was finishing up lighting the remaining wall scones.

She came to them, shaking her head. "I wanted you to know that I had already lighted the sconces on this floor. This is the second time in an hour I've done this."

"So someone else extinguished them?" he said, his gaze flicking to Mary.

Both females nodded.

"Thank you for telling us," he said, his face grim as he put his hand to Mary's waist and steered her toward the stairs.

"It seems I've been vindicated," she said softly.

"I never for a minute doubted your story. It's as clear as spring water that someone is desperate for your demise."

She shuddered.

Even before they reached the well-lit ground floor, they heard laughter coming from the eating room, where the Frenchmen had obviously returned to play cards. Stephen knocked upon the proprietor's door.

After two knocks, Becker answered, raising his bushy gray brows. "How may I be of service, my lord?"

Stephen spoke in a voice barely above a whisper. "We beg a word with you. In private."

Becker tossed a glance behind him, then stepped from the room, closing the door behind him.

"Will you come to my chamber?" Stephen asked.

"Yes, of course."

"There's a leak in the ceiling we should like you to see." It was a ruse, a lie, but Stephen wanted anyone who might be listening to think they were contacting the innkeeper on a maintenance matter.

As they climbed the stairs, no one spoke. When they reached

Stephen's room, he asked Becker to sit on the settle.

Becker looked up at the ceiling. "I see no signs of a leak."

"There is no leak. We needed to speak in private."

"Is this about the murder of your valet?" Becker asked. The man's entire demeanor had changed from one of jovial confidence to something cowering.

Murder could do that.

"That and the old woman's disappearance and . . . two attempts now on Lady Mary's life." Stephen glared at him.

Becker suddenly seemed older. Stephen would have guessed his age at sixty. The way he looked right now was closer to seventy. "I know nothing."

"You're lying." If only the man did not fear for his life, Stephen was certain he could get the truth from him. "I know you've helped the man or men responsible for these vile actions, and I also know you now fear for your own life, now that you know the person, or persons, you're aiding is capable of murder."

Becker's pale eyes flinched.

"The attempts on Lady Mary demonstrate this man—or men—will destroy anyone who has knowledge of the evil deeds. Lady Mary doesn't even know the identity of the killer, but he's determined to permanently silence her. What's to prevent him from doing the same to you? Or to your family?"

His eyes wide with fright, Becker swallowed hard.

"You and I together, along with Lady Mary, can stop them," Stephen said. "You and I are undoubtedly the largest men at Le Chateau. I'm skilled in pugilism and swords. And if we act swiftly, we'll have the element of surprise on our side. We can stop them, and we will!"

His breathing heavy, Becker gave no response.

"Our failure to act could result in more deaths." Stephen said. "How safe do you think your family is?"

The older man pondered this for a moment. Then he sighed. "I will help."

Mary moved to him and set a hand on his shoulder. "Please, tell us everything."

"It's the Frenchmen who arrived with you," he said, peering at Mary. "They gave me a large sum of money to help them. They needed something like a secret chamber in which to question the old woman, and they needed me to obliterate any signs that she'd ever been here. I had no trouble getting her chair men to hide in the hayloft and to persuade your chair men to deny the old woman's existence."

"So you paid them?" Mary said.

He nodded solemnly.

"And what of the journal stolen from my chamber?" Mary asked.

Becker's head inclined. He sucked in his breath. "That was me." He frowned. "They paid me to take it. It wasn't like taking your money, so I thought it harmless." He directed his gaze at her. "I beg your forgiveness."

"It doesn't signify now," she said. "What can you tell us about the Italians? Why is it they keep to themselves so much and pretend not to be able to speak French?"

"I have always prided myself on my discretion," Becker began. "The Italians know this. They come here because the gentleman is well known in his country. He travels with a false identity—and a false wife. The lovers leave their own spouses and come here twice a year. They have never mingled with other guests." He shrugged. "They avoid the risk of identification."

Stephen nodded, thankful Becker had been so forthcoming with information.

"Is Miss Willets . . . still alive?" Mary asked hopefully.

"I believe so."

"Where?" Stephen asked.

"There's a chamber on the ground floor directly beneath Room 1. It can be reached through a trap door in Room 1."

"That explains why the brothers both go into Room 1 each night," Stephen said. "Which makes it imperative we get Miss Willets out. Once they get the information they want from her, they'll kill her—if they haven't already."

Becker rose to his feet. "I have a key."

CHAPTER NINETEEN

T HEY HAD TO go through Becker's private chambers to reach the secret room. "Neither my wife nor my daughter know this room is being used, and I'm the only one with a key," he told Stephen and Mary.

When they came traipsing through the family's living quarters, Becker's rotund wife stared at them. "What are you doing?" she asked her husband in German.

For Mary, days of seeing nothing but endless mountains of snow had left her with no sense of where they were, but hearing Mrs. Becker speak in German made her wonder if they had reached the Tyrolean Alps, in which case, they might already be in Austria. She gave a silent prayer she'd live to see Sophia.

"I need to show something to our guests," Becker explained to his wife. "I told you we were privileged to be hosting an English lord and lady. This is them."

The woman dropped into a curtsy, her face transformed to something gleeful.

Mary inclined her head respectfully and told Mrs. Becker she was pleased to make her acquaintance.

"I may be a while," Becker explained to his wife. "Why don't you go ahead to bed, my darling?" He turned to Mary. "My wife rises at four each morning to start preparing the day's food."

Stephen said something in German to Becker's wife.

Mary watched with amusement as Mrs. Becker offered Stephen a broad smile. Of course she would. What woman could be immune to his considerable charms?

Mrs. Becker disappeared into what Mary presumed to be her bedchamber while they continued on to the secret room.

While Becker fiddled with the room's lock, Mary's stomach knotted. What if they were about to discover the murdered body of dear Miss Willets? She could hardly breathe.

"It's a good thing the Fontaine brothers are busy with their cards," Becker said. "They usually wait until bedtime before they come to the old woman."

With the lock off, Stephen eased open the door.

Mary drew in a deep breath.

The room was in total darkness. Becker went back to fetch a burning candle, and when he returned, they could clearly see into the chamber. Feet away from them a tall ladder reached to a trap door directly above it: the method of entry from Room 1. In the far corner, Miss Willets was tied to a chair. The woman was so still, Mary feared she was dead.

Mary moved closer, trembling with each shaky step. The older woman's mouth had been gagged, but her eyes appreciatively flashed with gladness when she saw Mary.

Mary rushed to her. "Thank God! You're alive." Mary set about untying the cloth that bound her mouth while Stephen used his penknife to cut through the ropes which bit so deeply into the flesh of her wrists they broke her skin. It sickened Mary to see that the woman's sleeves had been rolled up, and her arms were scarred with festering bruises. Those vile men had been torturing her.

"I am very grateful to you, my dear Lady Mary," Miss Willets said. In spite of all she had been through, Miss Willits' speech still held a cheerful note. "The French assassins cursed you mightily—which told me of your courage. How blessed I am that you did not remain complacent, that you stood up for me."

"We owe our gratitude to Lord Stephen Stanhope." Mary

bestowed a smile upon him.

He stepped forward.

"You, my dear lord, need no introduction. I believe we've communicated in the past," Miss Willets said.

"Then you *are* Miss Coney!"

"Indeed I am."

"I'm just so thankful you're still alive," Mary said.

"Me, too," Stephen added. "Why were you courting such danger? Could you not have sent a courier to London? Why so seriously jeopardize your own well-being?"

Miss Willets/Coney shook her head. "I had no reliable courier, and I possess vital information."

Stephen quirked a brow.

"Had I a trustworthy courier, I would have notified the Foreign Office that Napoleon is mounting an escape from Elba. But the really urgent matter that sent me on this perilous journey I could trust with no one." She suspiciously eyed Becker.

"You are with us?" Stephen asked the innkeeper.

"Absolutely."

Stephen nodded for Miss Willets to continue.

"A Frenchman attending the Congress of Vienna is not who he claims to be. He's an agent for Napoleon and will do everything in his power to sabotage all efforts of the delegation."

"Then it's imperative we get to Vienna. Soon," Stephen said.

"I shall have to entrust you with the information, Lord Stephen," Miss Willets said, sighing. "I'm afraid those horrid Frenchmen have broken my leg, and it will be too difficult for me to continue my journey at this time."

"How terrible!" Mary shrieked. "I'm so sorry you've had to endure so much."

"It's nothing that won't heal with time. A little rest is all I need. And it's not as if I didn't offer myself for these potentially dangerous missions. I knew there was a strong possibility I could be discovered. And killed. But thanks to you, my dear, my death now looks much less imminent." She turned to Stephen. "Now, what are we going to do about those assassins?"

"We'll do whatever it takes."

"But as a diplomat, you're not skilled in the field," the old woman said.

Stephen eyed Mary. "They've jeopardized what I hold dear. I'm just angry enough to do unto them what they would have done unto two defenseless females."

As he spoke, the trap door directly above the ladder squeaked open, flooding the chamber with more light.

CHAPTER TWENTY

S TEPHEN MOTIONED FOR the three of them to move to the room's darkest corner, where they stood against the wall and watched as a man's leg dangled down into the chamber.

"Say, Pierre, did you leave the candle burning down here last night?" the leg dangler asked. If he was speaking to Pierre, then this man must be Charles Fontaine.

Stephen held his breath while waiting for the other brother's response.

"You idiot! No candle could burn for that many hours."

The leg belonging to Charles Fontaine retreated back into the chamber above and, a moment later, the Frenchman's head poked into the chamber. The room wasn't dark enough to conceal Stephen, Mary, and Becker. The older brother then let out a stream of curses. "They've found the old woman!"

Stephen strained to hear the response. "It's not worth dying for. We need to get out of here."

Charles Fontaine leapt away and slammed the trap door shut.

Stephen and Becker exchanged glances. "Let's get them."

Becker nodded.

The two men started to leave the room. "No, please, Stephen," Mary said, "don't go. They might kill you."

He was touched by her concern, touched and relieved that she still must care for him. But cowardice was alien to him. He was duty bound to make these men pay for what they'd done to Humphrey. "Those men need to be stopped." He flashed a smile. "I shall be offended by your lack of confidence in me."

Before she could respond, he and Becker hurried back the same way they had entered. "I have a sword," Becker announced.

"I'm accounted to be skilled with the sword."

"Then you shall have mine."

Seconds later, Becker presented his sword to Stephen. Its quality was far less than what Stephen was accustomed to, but it was appreciated nonetheless. "You are armed with a knife?"

Becker nodded. "Always. One cannot be too careful."

Stephen hastened after Becker into the well-lighted reception area. Just before they reached the stairs, the Fontaine brothers' steps pounded on the stairs. Stephen drew his sword and came to plant one booted foot on the first step, awaiting the French assassins, a smirk on his face.

The Frenchmen stopped. All four men froze. A burning hatred boiled in Charles Fontaine's malevolent gaze. His knuckles whitened. Then he hurled his valise at Stephen with such force that it knocked Stephen backward.

Stephen pounced to his feet and just as he went to scoop the fallen sword from the floor, Pierre's foot came down on it. If the fellow had been smarter, he'd have tried to claim it for his own use.

What the devil was the man thinking, Stephen wondered. Pierre brandished no weapon as he faced Stephen, who was at least half a foot taller and a bit heavier. With one quick shove, Stephen knocked Pierre backward. The man crumpled into the stairs like a woman's fan. More French curses spewed.

Before he could retrieve his sword, Stephen caught sight of something shiny, and his gaze flitted to his right. Charles Fontaine lunged toward him, his dagger aimed directly at Stephen's heart. There wasn't enough time for Stephen to withdraw his own knife. He ducked into a squat and grabbed his attacker's ankles, forcing Charles to lose his balance and fall on top his brother as

Pierre was struggling to get up.

Mary moved into his peripheral vision less than ten feet away, holding the rope that must have bound Miss Willets. "Get away, Mary," he shouted.

"But I can tie them up for you."

"Go back," he said through gritted teeth, not removing his gaze from the brothers. He had unsheathed his knife and was engaged in a stare-down with the eldest brother. Charles' knife was significantly larger than Stephen's, and Stephen was well aware that these men had significantly more practice than he in fighting until death. His heartbeat drummed. His palms were sweaty. He'd be lying if he said he wasn't scared.

He wanted to pick up the sword, but that brief pause is all it would take for one of the brothers to kill him.

Becker came to stand at his left, his knife drawn and, uncharacteristically, spoke in German. "I'll go after the one on the left."

The Frenchmen obviously did not understand what Becker had said.

When Becker launched at Pierre, Stephen would go for his brother. If he did not succeed, Charles Fontaine would. And Stephen would die. Stephen had the advantage of being younger and quicker than his opponent, but the older man was undoubtedly more experienced in lethal fights.

Rather than mounting a deadly offensive, it was far more palatable to Stephen to defend himself by ridding his opponent of that menacing dagger. It would have been far easier had he the sword that lay at his feet, but getting it now was out of the question.

Becker lunged at Pierre, but Pierre twirled away. He managed to knick Becker's hand with his knife. Blood spurted.

Stephen's six-inch knife struck the other man's foot-long knife, but Charles' grip held. Stephen's hopes of dislodging the dagger died. Stephen retreated, careful not to get backed into the wall. As Charles came after him, Stephen knew his rival would be at a disadvantage going upstairs backward, so he lunged toward him, aiming his knife for the other man's heart. Even if he missed, he would force the man to retreat backward. The older brother was quicker than expected. He took two steps—backward—in order to avoid being stabbed.

Charles stared at Stephen, a sadistic look on his bronzed face.

Mary moved closer. Of course the exasperating girl hadn't done what Stephen had asked her to do. She bent and picked up the sword. As much as he wanted it, he wasn't about to flinch from Charles Fontaine's sinister gaze. It could be the last thing he ever did.

"The English lord is too soft," Charles said, sneering.

"Of course he is," Mary said in French, moving toward the elder Fontaine brother. "He's not a killer like you."

"Get out of here, Mary!" Stephen shouted angrily, his eyes never leaving Charles Fontaine. "Why did you murder my valet?"

"The man saw too much."

Stephen's brows lowered. "From his garret room?"

"No. That fool Becker failed to close the door to the secret room after he brought food to the old woman, and the valet saw her when he assisted Becker's wife with a barrel of wine."

So Humphrey's helpful nature resulted in his death. What tragic irony.

Instead of obeying Stephen, Mary raised the sword and it came down on Charles' dagger, dislodging it.

But at great cost.

The man leapt to her, his muscular arm circling her neck. He easily took the sword away, and still choke holding her, pointed the sword to her breastbone, and eyed Stephen. "Put down your knife, or I'll kill her."

Stephen's knife dropped to the wooden floor.

Charles looked at Becker. "You, too."

Becker let go of his knife.

The door to Becker's private chambers banged open, and there stood Mrs. Becker, directing a musket at the Frenchmen. Becker spoke to her in German, then addressed Charles Fontaine.

"If you don't release the lady, my wife will blow a hole through your brother."

Charles' gaze darted to his brother. He showed no emotion but stood there for a moment, analyzing his options. After a moment, he released his hold on Mary and shoved her down the stairs. She lost her balance and plummeted to the floor.

As much as Stephen wanted to assist her, he wasn't about to remove his gaze from these killers. Fortunately, she must not have sustained any injuries because she got to her feet and came to stand just behind him.

Mrs. Becker spoke to her husband, and he translated. "My wife said if you don't leave Le Chateau right now, she will kill one of you. You may get your valises, but the knives stay."

"But our chair men can't travel at night," Charles protested.

"Who said anything about chair men?" Becker asked. "You'll not risk their lives. You've already killed one man too many."

Stephen held his breath. Either way, these men would die.

The brothers exchanged terrified glances. Charles nodded, then picked up his valise.

Stephen picked up his knife, stepped back to allow them to pass, and watched cautiously as Pierre moved down the four steps and picked up his valise from the ground where it had landed after he'd hurled it at Stephen. His brother followed, and the two grim-faced men strode to the inn's door and left.

Becker rushed to lock the door. "That's the end of those evil men."

FROM THEIR PERCH at the eating room window, Mary and Stephen watched the Brothers Fontaine trudge through snow. Taking the path started by the chair men, they soon reached the largest cottage and began to bang on the door.

Becker came up behind them. "When I knew those men were

responsible for your valet's death, I made my way to that cottage and warned the chair men against the Frenchmen. They won't be helping those killers."

Indeed, the Fontaines pounded and pounded upon the cottage door, but no one came. The men's shouts could be heard at the inn some eighty yards away. Were they so foolish they didn't realize there would be no rescue for them?

Eventually, they gave up and tried the other outbuildings, each of which was locked. Their efforts to gain entrance yielded nothing. Finally, they set off on foot. The snowfall had lessened considerably from what it had been days earlier, but the snow's depth still had not diminished. With each step, the men sank into knee-high snow. Even though the men wore substantial fur-lined boots, Mary shuddered just imagining how cold their feet must be. She recalled how miserable she'd been while the chair men carried her along the mountain paths, her ill-shod feet dangling.

Whatever catastrophe awaited those men was well deserved. They'd viciously murdered Humphrey, and Mary had no doubts they planned to kill Miss Willets once they were through with her. And twice, they had tried to kill Mary.

"The fact they're not armed makes one rest easier," Stephen said.

"We need not worry they'll hurt anyone else," Becker said. "In eight hours, they will be dead."

Mary felt a chill climb up her spine. Becker, who'd lived in these mountains all his life, would know about such things. Oddly, she felt not a shred of guilt over these men's fates. They had brought it on themselves with their wickedness.

"Poor Humphrey," Stephen said, his voice forlorn.

"When spring comes, I will see that your servant is properly buried," Becker pledged.

Stephen turned to him and offered a handshake. "You're a good man, Becker. Thank you for everything."

"And so is your good wife," Mary added.

"I'd best go explain everything to her." Becker started for his private chambers.

"We must go to Miss Willets," Mary said.

They installed Miss Willets, or Miss Coney, in Mary's chamber because a fire had been built there and because Mary felt she should look after her this first night. Becker had produced the woman's portmanteau, and Mary gave her the furry boots.

"I won't be leaving here until spring, and I doubt I'll need them then. I want you to have them, Lady Mary." Miss Willets then turned to Stephen. "The chair men will know better than anyone when it will be safe to continue on your journey. You must hurry on to Vienna as soon as you're able. You know Lord Castlereagh, do you not?"

"Very well."

"Good. You must tell him everything. About Napoleon's escape. And about Monsieur Laurent who is trusted by Tallyrand but a minion of Boney's. He means to undermine the work of the Congress."

"What about you?" Mary asked her.

"Our government has seen to it that my efforts are well funded. My chair men will be compensated for staying here during my convalescence." With a smile on her face, the old woman gave a satisfied sigh. "Then it will be my pleasure to return to England— for good. I'm too old for this."

AFTER MARY DRESSED the following morning, she looked out the window and was pleased to observe her chair men completing the digging of a path to the inn's front door. But she was even more pleased that not a single flake of snow was falling.

Miss Willets rose up in the bed, not without wincing in pain.

Mary faced her. "Should you like me to procure you a cup of nice, hot tea?"

"That would be lovely. You know what my tin looks like."

Mary had never thought to see either Miss Willets or her tea tin ever again. She found it with the woman's things and went to the eating room. With the absence of the Frenchmen and daylight streaming into the chamber, the oppressive mood at Le Chateau had lifted, and it now seemed a joyous place.

Stephen, who'd returned to their old table, stood when she entered. Their shining eyes met. For that moment, she felt as if she were drowning in happiness yet buoyed by it at the same time. All the darkness was behind them.

Once she was seated, the braided blonde brought steaming water for the tea and offered to take Miss Willets' to her.

Stephen placed a hand over Mary's. His touch affected her like champagne. "Becker said we're but a couple of days away from Vienna," he said.

If one could drown of happiness, she was well on her way. To think, she'd soon see Sophia, soon dance the Viennese waltz. Who knows? She might even meet the Duke of Wellington.

Most of all, she was grateful for Stephen. Even though he'd only been interested in her welfare to satisfy her brother, she knew she had come to mean a great deal to Stephen. There was no doubt he would have given his life to protect her.

"And the blizzards, I believe, are behind us," she said.

"Indeed. We're to leave tomorrow." He stroked her forearm and lowered his voice. "I missed you in my bed last night."

His words sent her insides flipping like pilchards in a net. "I'll not be repeating such a foolish action."

"There's nothing foolish about such an action," he said, his voice low and husky. "Not when the man is in love with the woman."

He'd said it! He really did love her. He wasn't just acting nobly to please Devere. Likely for the first time in her life, Mary was bereft of words—an exceedingly rare occurrence.

He turned his chair to face her squarely. "This is neither the place nor the manner in which I'd thought to have this conversation."

Her brows came together. "What conversation?"

"The one in which I tell you that even though you're a disaster on your surroundings with your supreme untidiness, even though you are prone to . . . exaggerate the truth, even though you're impulsive to the point of idiocy, even though you're the most maddening woman I've ever known, I could traipse the world over and never find a woman possessed of a bigger heart or a deeper sense of honor, nor could I ever find anyone else with whom I'd rather spend the rest of my life."

Her heart felt as if it were weeping with joy. "Are you saying . . . asking what I think you're asking?"

"I'm asking if you would honor me by becoming my wife. I do love you most sincerely."

Even though this was unquestionably the happiest moment of her life, she decided to make him squirm. "I would consider accepting, but you must retract your statement where you described me with the word *idiocy*."

He burst into laughter. "Forgive me, maddening woman."

Nothing she could say to him could match his eloquence—except for the bit about *idiocy*. "Very well, but I'm not going to launch into flowery prose about how deeply I love you. I've already made a cake of myself in that respect."

"Never that, my darling. No woman has ever been more beautiful or more loved than that night when you revealed your feelings toward me."

"It was a lovely night."

"The first of many."

And even though their fellow travelers were watching, Stephen leaned over and kissed her firmly.

EPILOGUE

T HIS WAS THE night of their first ball in Vienna. How Stephen was looking forward to displaying his beautiful wife for all his fellow diplomats to see. Her beauty in the soft violet gown had left him gaping and speechless. "I wish, my dearest wife, I had one of the Lancaster jewels to clasp about your lovely neck." He came to her and nibbled at the silken skin where her neck met her shoulders.

"All the adornment I need is having you next to me," she murmured. "You will be the most handsome man at his lordship's ball. All the women will be eager to dance with one as tall as you."

Grinning, he shook his head as he put his hand to her waist and steered her from their bedchamber at the Birminghams' lavish residence.

Downstairs, Will and Sophia Birmingham awaited. It was clear to him the former Beresford sisters would be the loveliest woman in attendance tonight. Though the sisters did not resemble—Sophia being possessed of dark hair and Mary of blonde—they were both stunning.

"You two have certainly been busy since you arrived yesterday," Will said to the newly married Stanhopes. "First, foiling one of Boney's evil plots . . ."

"Then getting the embassy to approve your marriage and

finding a British clergyman to marry you," Sophia finished.

Mary came to hug her sister. "I'm just so happy you were able to stand up with us at that altar. You and Will. It made for a perfect day."

The Birmingham coach, which was fit for royalty, carried them to Lord Castlereagh's ball where Stephen's wife was greatly admired.

But the highlight of the night came when Lord Castlereagh and the Duke of Wellington—whom Mary gushed over—invited him and his bride to his lordship's library.

"We wanted both of you here because the offer we're making will affect you both," the duke said.

Stephen nodded. *Offer?* He could not imagine what was going to be offered.

"In light of your exemplary service," Lord Castlereagh said, "which, I understand, came at great peril to your life, we wish to reward you. During these years you've provided such faithful service to the crown, you've never denied that you would one day wish to have your own ambassadorship."

"That's true," Stephen said, his heart pounding with excitement. *Please, though, not some cold post like Russia.*

"Therefore," the duke said, "we wish to offer you Naples."

Stephen whirled to his bride. Naples had always been his first choice, and early in their acquaintance, Mary had said she, too, felt the lure of that ancient Italian kingdom. She broke into a wide, open smile.

He took her hand and squeezed it before returning his attention to his country's two highest-ranking diplomats. "We most heartily accept."

Later, he and Mary found a quiet corner. "Because of you, all my dreams have come true," he told her.

She shook her head. "Not me. Devere."

He nodded knowingly. "I owe him everything."

Author's Notes

Since I have always loved to play the "What if" game, I asked myself how a Regency heroine could get enmeshed in a perilous situation like that of the heroine of Ethel Lina White's 1936 mystery novel *The Wheel Spins*, which Alfred Hitchcock adapted into his 1938 class *The Lady Vanishes*. The result is *Lady Mary's Dangerous Encounter*, the book you've just read. I hope you enjoyed it, and I hope you'll want to read the next book in the series, *My Lord Protector*, in which Lady Mary's powerful brother, Devere, stars.

–Cheryl Bolen

About the Author

Since her first book was published to acclaim in 1998, Cheryl Bolen has written more than three dozen Regency-set historical romances. Several of her books have won Best Historical awards, and she's a *New York Times* and *USA Today* bestseller as well as an Amazon All Star whose books have been translated into nine languages. She's also been penning articles about Regency England and giving workshops on the era for more than twenty years.

In previous lives, she was a journalist and an English teacher. She's married to a recently retired college professor, and they're the parents of two grown sons, both of whom she says are brilliant and handsome! All four Bolens (and their new daughter-in-law) love to travel to England, and Cheryl loves college football and basketball and adores reading letters and diaries penned by long-dead Englishwomen.

Check out these sites of hers:
subscribe to newsletter – littl.ink/newsletter
blog – blogl.ink/RegencyRamblings
website – www.CherylBolen.com
facebook – fbl.ink/Facebook
Pinterest – littl.ink/Pinterest
Readers' group – facebook.com/groups/2586590498319473

CPSIA information can be obtained
at www.ICGtesting.com
Printed in the USA
BVHW090916120122
625991BV00013B/687

9 781956 003031